KEVIN HASLAM

The Quiet Parts

Short Stories

First published by Calling Field Press 2026

Copyright © 2026 by Kevin Haslam

All rights reserved. No part of this publication may be reproduced, stored, or transmitted in any form or by any means, electronic, mechanical, photocopying, recording, scanning, or otherwise without written permission from the publisher. It is illegal to copy this book, post it to a website, or distribute it by any other means without permission.

This novel is entirely a work of fiction. The names, characters, and incidents portrayed in it are the work of the author's imagination. Any resemblance to actual persons, living or dead, events, or localities is entirely coincidental.

Kevin Haslam asserts the moral right to be identified as the author of this work.

The author is grateful to the following publications for first publishing earlier versions of these stories:

An earlier version of "Every Cell Screams" appeared in Dime Show Review, Volume 3, Issue 1 (2019).

An early version of "Drowning Carnations," originally titled "Refuse," appeared in Adelaide: Independent Literary Magazine, No. 25 (June 2019).

"Auld Lang Syne" was previously published in You Forgot About Me (short story collection, November 2, 2018).

An early version of "Approved Gray," originally titled "Luminous Vestige" was previously published in The Inner Life of Shifting (short story collection, August 22, 2020).

"Spitting Distance" originally appeared in The Magnolia Review, Volume 5, Issue 1 (January 2019).

First edition

ISBN: 978-1-7323668-8-6

Cover art by Yoonie Co.

*This book was professionally typeset on Reedsy.
Find out more at reedsy.com*

For Jack and Andy, who keep the lights on.
For Nicole, my co-conspirator, my constant.
For Mookie, my very best friend.

"I do not ask the wounded person how he feels, I myself become the wounded person."

WALT WHITMAN "SONG OF MYSELF," 33

Contents

Prologue	1
INTAKE	3
SECURITY DEPOSIT	20
BOUNDARY LINE	34
CIVIL SERVANT	48
APPROVED GRAY	50
CONGRATULATIONS	58
PERMISSION	69
MENDED	85
SPITTING DISTANCE	95
DROWNING CARNATIONS	101
EVERY CELL SCREAMS	107
REWIND	115
"AULD LANG SYNE"	118
RESOLVED	125
OPEN MIC	132
THE BALLROOM	143
THE WEIGHT OF SOUND	146
INTERLUDE	155
THE SOUNDTRACK OF THE IN-BETWEEN	156
Track-list	158
Liner Notes	159
SIDE A — THE WAITING ROOM	160
Track 01 — Tiny House Theory	161

Track 02 — Halo	169
Track 03 — Number Three	175
Track 04 — Why Am I Not the One	181
Track 05 — Inkwell	187
Track 06 — Next to Nowhere	194
SIDE B — TERMS & LIGHT	200
Track 07 — VIP Black Gucci	201
Track 08 — Turn Around	208
Track 09 — Streetlight Secrets	214
Track 10 — New Jersey & Florida	220
Track 11 — Frozen Desire	227
Track 12 — Failing Heart	232
(HIDDEN TRACK)	238
About the Author	242

Prologue

If you're reading this, you've already done something most people don't.

You stopped.

Not in a dramatic way. Nothing cinematic. You just paused long enough to let a page hold your attention. That's rare now. Attention costs more than money.

These stories aren't built for speed. They're not interested in big twists or clean answers. They live in the places where life usually keeps moving: the waiting room chair that sits slightly wrong, the kitchen table that becomes a court, the bar where "community" is an excuse, the motel morning where your phone stays quiet and still manages to speak.

I'm drawn to the moments that don't look like moments until you're past them. The soft pivot where a person realizes they've been shrinking. The second before someone says, "I can't keep holding this," and means it. The quiet calculation of whether it's safer to tell the truth or to make it sound easier to hear.

If there's a villain in this book, it isn't a single person. It's the way we're trained to treat one another like a problem to process. The way systems ask for "one more thing" until you disappear. The way a room laughs because laughter is cheaper than responsibility. The way love can become a series of small postponements—soon, after this run, when things settle—until "soon" starts to feel like a threat.

But I don't think this is a hopeless book.

I think it's a book about staying human in places that don't make it easy. About the small mercies we offer when we're tired. About the ways we fail and the ways we choose, sometimes, not to.

You don't have to read this quickly. You don't have to read it all at once. I wrote it for the part of you that notices what everyone else steps over.

The quiet parts.

Thank you for being here.

INTAKE

The clinic had been built with the sort of optimism that didn't survive contact with budgets.

A municipal seal was bolted above the door—blue enamel, flaking at the edges—like a promise made in a past administration and forgotten in a meeting. Inside, the heat ran too high in winter and too low in summer. The waiting room chairs were molded plastic on scuffed metal legs, all of them angled slightly wrong, as though the building itself discouraged you from settling. Mara sat behind the intake desk under fluorescent lights that made everyone look as though they were being questioned by the ceiling.

The desk was laminated faux wood, its edges rounded like a school desk. A pane of Plexiglas divided her from the room. Someone had taped signs on both sides of the window: PLEASE HAVE YOUR ID READY. MASKS REQUIRED. NO FOOD OR DRINK. Another sign, printed in soft fonts, said WE SEE YOU. WE CARE. A small sticker of a cartoon sloth sat beneath it, smiling around a heart like it had never needed anything. Mara kept her hands flat on the counter when she wasn't typing. It made her look calm. It stopped her from tapping out her impatience. She was good at looking calm. That was part of why she'd been hired: not vocation, exactly—more a talent for absorbing other people's urgency without catching fire.

A clock hung above the water cooler. Its second hand swept with confidence. The minute hand crept in small, unreliable increments. On her screen, the day's list glowed. It was never accurate. People came early, people came late, people came without appointments, people came with paperwork folded into quarters and softened by rain. The city had renamed the place twice in the last decade, trying to make it sound less like what it was: a clinic that existed where private care didn't, and an intake desk where the world's spillage pooled.

* * *

A line formed as soon as Mara unlocked the sliding window. The first three were regulars: a man who recited his birthday like a dare, a teenage girl with a cough that sounded held back, a woman who handed over documents as though she were laying down weapons.

Mara typed and clicked and nodded. She asked the same questions in a voice that tried to sound like a person. She watched the waiting room because waiting rooms had rules. The corner near the outlet was always taken. The chairs nearest the door were avoided. Children were sticky in ways no one admitted. When Mara looked up again, she saw her. Not immediately—nothing about the woman demanded recognition. Her face lived behind other faces.

But Mara's mind had filed it away under Recurring, the way a clerk filed a form. The woman stood two places back in line, holding a folder that had been too many times in a too-small bag. Her hair was twisted into a knot that wouldn't last the day.

She wore a thin jacket with a broken zipper, and she held the folder to her chest with both hands, as though it were something fragile and borrowed. A child stood beside her, or half behind her: a boy of about four, cheeks chapped red. He leaned into her leg with his head turned away from the room, thumb at his mouth. He had the weary look children got when they learned the world asked questions and took too long to answer. Something in Mara clicked—not pity, exactly. More the recognition of a pattern about to repeat, and the requirement that she pretend it wasn't one. The woman reached the window. Mara slid it open.

"Hi," the woman said. Her voice was careful.

She didn't lead with anger or apology, though apology lived under her words like a folded note. She said her name and then her son's and offered the folder. Mara took it. The papers inside were arranged neatly. There was the intake form.

Proof of residency. Pay stubs, stapled. An immunization record printed faintly, ink a little smeared, like the printer had been running out of itself. What she didn't have, Mara suspected, was the one thing that would make all of it count. Mara clicked into the woman's file. The gray administrative header appeared. Under Notes were four short entries, the clinic's official voice turning a person into "patient" and weeks into date stamps.

11/07: PATIENT PRESENTED FOR PEDIATRIC VISIT, MISSING PHOTO ID.

PROVIDED LIST OF ACCEPTABLE DOCUMENTATION.

11/14: PATIENT PRESENTED, PROVIDED ID, MISSING PROOF OF INCOME.

PROVIDED LIST.

11/21: PATIENT PRESENTED, PROVIDED INCOME, MISSING PROOF OF RESIDENCY.

PROVIDED LIST.

11/28: PATIENT PRESENTED, PROVIDED RESIDENCY, MISS-ING CUSTODY

DOCUMENTATION / GUARDIANSHIP FORM. PROVIDED LIST.

Mara read them quickly, though she knew them already. They made it look as though something had been solved each time. Provided list. Provided list. Provided list. She looked up. The woman smiled in a way that said, I did it. I listened. I'm trying.

"Okay," Mara said, letting her voice soften without turning sweet. "Let's take a look." The woman nodded fast. She hitched her son higher on her hip. The boy's eyes flicked to Mara's face and away, as though eye contact might incur a fee. Mara flipped through the folder again, slower, allowing herself one second of hope that the missing thing had appeared, the way you sometimes found a coin in a couch cushion. "What do you have for guardianship?" Mara asked. The woman's smile wavered.

"I brought his birth certificate. It's a copy—the one they gave me. I have it." Her hands moved quickly, finding the paper as if speed could make it more official. She slid it under the window. Mara saw the boy's name. The woman's name. The seal. The language. She saw that it was not, by the clinic's standards, enough. Mara clicked again, keeping her face from changing in a way that would make the woman brace.

"We just need one more thing," Mara said, because those were the words the job gave you, the gentle hinge between wanting to help and being designed not to. The woman's shoulders dropped in a motion small enough to pass for breath. Mara had seen it before: the body preparing for disappointment while still standing upright. "The guardianship form," Mara continued. "Or something showing you're listed on his insurance as parent. If the father is also—"

"It's just me," the woman said too quickly. "It's been just me. I mean, he's... he's not—" She stopped, swallowed, caught herself mid-truth. "I'm his mom. That's my name." Mara could see the week-by-week assembling behind the woman's eyes: RIPTA bus trips, hours off work that weren't really off, favors owed, the belief that if you did what the paper demanded, the door would open.

"Okay," Mara said. "I understand. We have an affidavit form here you can fill out." The woman blinked.

"I can do that."

Mara hesitated, because she knew the next sentence and she hated it. "It has to be notarized." The woman stared at her.

In the waiting room, a child began to cry. Someone's phone played a tinny song through cheap speakers. The fluorescent lights flickered faintly.

"Notarized," the woman repeated, as if it were a word that might become doable if she said it enough times.

"Yeah," Mara said. "There's a bank down the street that—"

"I don't have a bank," the woman said, and there was no drama in it, just the flatness of fact. "They told me last time—about the bank. But I went, and they said it costs money, and I—" She stopped again. Her cheeks flushed, as if the sentence I don't have money were impolite. "I tried the library. They said they don't do it." Mara nodded.

"Sometimes community centers—"

"I work," the woman cut in, and a sharp edge surfaced before she could smooth it away. "I have a job. I'm not—" She looked down at her son and the sharpness softened into something strained. "He has a fever at night. He's been coughing. He needs—" Her voice cracked on needs.

"We can still see him as a walk-in," Mara heard herself say, because some part of her couldn't bear the thought of sending the woman away empty-handed. "But for enrollment and reduced-cost services, we need the affidavit notarized." The woman's eyes widened a fraction, as if this were a small mercy offered at a toll booth.

"Okay," she said quickly.

"Okay, so… we can do the walk-in?" Mara typed, hunting for an appointment slot that didn't exist. "There's a wait," she said. "A few hours, possibly."

"That's fine," the woman said, with a kind of brutal optimism. "We'll wait."

Mara printed the affidavit form and a list of notary locations. She slid the papers under the window. The woman took them and looked at them as if they were a map in a language she couldn't read.

"Is there—" the woman began. She leaned closer to the Plexiglas, as if closeness could create an exception. "Is there anything else I can do? Like, is there a way to just—" She made a vague gesture, indicating the missing notary like a loose screw. For a second, Mara imagined saying, Yes. I can stamp it myself. I can pretend I watched you sign. I can be the witness you need. The thought wasn't heroic. It was simply tired.

"Not today," Mara said gently. "But if you come back with this notarized, we can get everything set." The woman nodded, swallowing something.

"Okay. Okay." She turned away from the desk, folder clutched tight again, and sat near the wall. She positioned her son on her lap so his small body fit against hers like he belonged there.

Mara watched them a beat too long. Then she slid the window closed and turned back to the line. By noon, the waiting room was full. A man argued softly about a missed appointment. A woman slept sitting up, her arms wrapped around herself. A toddler crawled under chairs until he bumped someone and wailed. The air smelled like disinfectant failing to keep up. Mara drank water in quick gulps between patients, as if she were trying to keep a small fire from spreading.

Around one, her supervisor appeared behind her desk. Darlene had tidy hair that suggested sleep. She carried a clipboard like a badge.

"How's it going?" Darlene asked, though the question wasn't real.

"Busy," Mara said, still typing. Darlene leaned against the counter, looking out at the waiting room as if it were a weather report.

"We've had some complaints," she said. Mara's fingers paused.

"About what?"

"Tone," Darlene said briskly. "Not you specifically. Just... generally. People feel dismissed." Mara almost laughed. The chairs and the signs dismissed people by existing.

Darlene tapped her clipboard. "Remember the script," she said. "Validate, redirect. People want to feel heard even when the answer's no."

"Right," Mara said.

"And don't bend rules because someone is persistent," Darlene added, like a line from training. "That's how we get audited."

The afternoon dragged. Mara's mind did what it always did on days like this: it split. One part stayed on the surface—smiling, typing, asking questions. Another floated above, watching her like a stranger. The floating part kept a tally of small injuries: the father turned away because he lacked a utility bill, the woman crying quietly because her insurance had lapsed, the teenager who flinched when asked if she felt safe at home.

And, in the corner, the mother with the folder. Every so often the woman rose and approached the desk to ask a small clarifying question, not to argue but to search for the right phrasing. Each time, Mara gave the same answer. Each time, the woman nodded and returned to her chair with a slightly dimmer face.

By three, the boy's feverish flush was visible even from behind Plexiglas. The woman's eyes were red-rimmed. She had the look of someone trying not to cry in a place where crying felt like failure. When she stood again, she moved slower, as if her body was reluctant to rehearse the ritual one more time.

Mara slid the window open.

"Hi," the woman said. Her voice was thin. "They said he can't be seen today. They said the walk-in list is full." Mara's stomach sank. She checked the schedule. The clinician who handled pediatrics had called out sick. The replacement provider had filled every slot.

"I'm sorry," Mara said. The words tasted like dust. "We don't have any more walk-in capacity today." The woman's face tightened.

"But he's sick."

"I know," Mara said, and hated how it sounded like a platitude.

"If it's urgent, if he has trouble breathing, if his fever is high—you should go to the emergency room."

"The ER bills me," the woman said, and the edge in her voice sharpened. "They send it to collections. They call. They...I can't..." She swallowed hard. "I can't do that again." Again. Mara's mind snagged on it. Again meant history. Again meant the woman had already been punished for being in need.

Mara inhaled slowly.

"Do you have a primary care provider?"

"That's why I'm here," the woman said.

Mara wanted to ask, How do you keep coming back? Not because she doubted her, but because Mara couldn't imagine carrying that kind of persistence without breaking.

"There's urgent care on Maple," Mara offered. "They have a sliding scale sometimes."

"I went," the woman said. "They said they don't take kids without insurance."

Mara closed her eyes for a fraction of a second. The training videos did not include this part: the part where every door someone suggested had already been tried and found locked. She opened her eyes and looked at the woman.

"What's your name again?" she asked, though she already knew.

The woman blinked, surprised.

"Elena," she said.

"Elena Ramirez." Mara said it silently, like a spell. Elena Ramirez. A name that deserved to be more than a file. "And your son?"

"Mateo." The woman's voice softened on his name. Mateo stood beside her now, too tired to be shy. He leaned against the desk, his head on his arm. His breath came in small, raspy pulls. Mara's chest tightened.

"Okay," Mara said, and heard her voice change, become more human. "Okay. Let me… let me see what I can do." Darlene's voice echoed in her mind—Don't bend rules because someone is persistent—and another voice, older and quieter, whispered: We can't keep telling people to come back with one more thing until they disappear. Mara turned back to her computer. She clicked into Elena's file, into the section that held the guardianship requirement.

The system was rigid in the way only bureaucracies could be. It didn't care about context. It cared about boxes. Under Guardianship Documentation was a drop-down:

AFFIDAVIT NOTARIZED.

COURT ORDER.

FOSTER PLACEMENT.

OTHER.

Mara hovered over Other. In the notes field she could type anything. The system would accept it. It would accept a lie as long as it was formatted correctly. She felt her pulse in her fingertips.

"Mara," Elena said softly, as if afraid to interrupt. "If there's no way—"

"Just a second," Mara said without looking up. She clicked Other. A box opened:

Please specify.

Her fingers hovered. She thought of audits and policies. She thought of Mateo's face and his small body pressed into his mother as if she were the only reliable structure in the world. She typed:

Birth certificate provided. Mother present. Relationship confirmed.

Vague enough to feel like truth. Also not what policy demanded. A red icon appeared:

DOCUMENTATION INCOMPLETE.

Mara's jaw clenched. She knew why: the system required a scanned notarized affidavit to complete enrollment. But there was a workaround. There was always a workaround, because systems were built by humans and humans left escape hatches for themselves.

She clicked into a different tab:

Temporary Coverage / Emergency Enrollment.

It was meant for crises, immediate care while paperwork was processed. It allowed a thirty-day provisional status. It required staff attestation. A checkbox appeared:

Staff confirms documentation will be obtained within 30 days.

Mara stared at it. The checkbox was the escape hatch. It wasn't advertised to patients. It wasn't offered at the window. It existed so staff could make the system look compassionate without changing it. Mara could check it. She could enroll Mateo temporarily and get him seen, get him what he needed. She could buy time. She also knew, because of whispered conversations in the break room, what followed. Temporary coverage triggered automatic referrals. It flagged a family as "high need." It opened other doors. Doors that didn't always lead to help. If Mara checked it, the system would generate a case in the city's Family Support Network. A case manager would be assigned. On paper, that sounded like resources. It also meant Elena's file would be shared across departments: billing, compliance, sometimes even the law enforcement liaison if there were concerns about fraud or neglect. It meant Elena's life would become legible to strangers with authority.

Mara thought of Elena stopping herself mid-sentence earlier, careful not to say too much. People learned to speak in fragments around systems that punished full disclosure. Mara swallowed hard. She could feel the moral injury in her throat, like a bruise. She looked up. Elena watched her through the Plexiglas, eyes wide with the kind of hope that made Mara want to be careful with it. Mateo leaned against his mother, eyelids drooping, his body giving up in small ways.

Mara clicked the checkbox. Elena's eyes widened slightly.

"We can put Mateo into temporary enrollment," Mara said, choosing each word. "It means we can get him seen. It gives us thirty days to get the notarized affidavit. Yes?" she asked.

Elena's expression shifted—relief, quick and bright, like a match in the dark.

"Yes. I can get it. I can—I can figure it out."

Mara nodded and slid a form under the window.

"Sign here," she said. "It acknowledges the temporary status and that you'll bring the affidavit." Elena took the pen with trembling fingers. Her hand shook as she signed, as if her body didn't fully trust mercy. Mara watched the signature appear—black ink on white paper. A simple curve of letters. A name becoming consent. Mara signed too, in the staff attestation line. Her own signature, practiced and fast. She signed dozens of forms a day. This one felt heavier, as if she'd dipped her pen into consequence.

Elena handed the form back and exhaled a sound that might have been a laugh or a sob.

"Thank you," Elena said. "Thank you so much. I was—I didn't know what to do." Mara nodded, feeling a strange hollowness.

"We'll get him seen," she said. "You'll need to wait a bit, but we can add him."

Elena pulled Mateo close, murmuring to him in Spanish—words Mara didn't catch but understood anyway: We're okay. They're going to help. Mateo leaned into her, eyes closing. Elena turned back to Mara, gratitude open and unguarded.

"You're... you're really kind," she said. The compliment landed like a stone. Kind. Mara had been trained to be kind the way you handled hazardous materials: with distance, with gloves.

"Just doing my job," Mara said automatically.

"No." Elena shook her head. "You didn't have to." Mara didn't know what to say to that. The truth was she did have to, if she wanted to keep living with herself. And the other truth was she had set something in motion Elena couldn't see. Elena returned to her seat, clutching the folder now like a trophy instead of a shield.

Mara turned back to her screen. The system processed the temporary enrollment. A green check mark appeared beside Mateo's name. Under Status, it read:

TEMP ACTIVE.

Another window popped up automatically:

Referral generated: Family Support Network. Case manager to be assigned.

Mara stared at the notification. It was the machine's way of saying, Thank you for feeding me. Here is what I will do now. She clicked it away. The green check mark remained. The next patient stepped up. Mara slid open the window. She asked the next set of questions. She smiled. She typed. She kept her voice cool without letting it go cold. Inside, something had shifted. A small fracture, or a widening crack—Mara couldn't tell which. Later, in the lull between rushes, she stood and walked to the back hallway where staff kept coats and half-eaten lunches.

The hallway smelled faintly of microwaved soup and hand sanitizer. She leaned against the wall and closed her eyes. She thought of the referral. She had seen what happened when families were routed into "support." Sometimes it was help: food vouchers, childcare subsidies, housing lists. Sometimes it was a net with hooks: mandatory meetings, documentation demands, compliance threats. A case manager could be a lifeline or a leash. It depended on who was assigned. It depended on how notes were interpreted. It depended on what the system needed to prove it was doing something.

Mara imagined Elena receiving a phone call from a case manager she didn't ask for. She imagined Elena's careful speech. She imagined a note in the file:

Patient difficult to reach. Non-compliant with documentation.

Non-compliant. A word that turned struggle into sin.

Mara opened her eyes and went back to the desk. Darlene appeared again around five, when the waiting room had thinned and the air felt stale with everyone's patience.

"How'd it go with that Ramirez situation?" Darlene asked, casually, as if asking about the weather. Mara's hands paused over the keyboard. She could lie. She could say Elena left. She could say nothing changed.

Instead she said, "I did a temporary enrollment." Darlene's eyebrows lifted.

"You did?"

"The boy needed to be seen. We didn't have walk-in capacity, but I got him in on the last slot." Darlene's mouth tightened, not quite displeased, not quite approving.

"That's... creative," she said. "Did you use the script?"

Mara almost laughed.

"I told her I could see she worked hard," Mara said, because that was the part Darlene cared about. "I said I understood it was frustrating." Darlene nodded, satisfied.

"Good. That matters."

"You know temporary enrollment triggers follow-up," Mara said carefully.

Darlene waved a hand.

"That's fine. That's what it's there for. We connect families to resources. That's the whole point." Mara felt heat rise in her throat.

"Sometimes the follow-up is... complicated." Darlene's gaze sharpened a fraction.

"We can't control what other departments do," she said, and her voice turned official "Our responsibility is to provide care and follow protocol. If there's a referral, that means the family qualifies for support." Qualifies. The word made Mara want to grind her teeth. Darlene leaned closer, lowering her voice as if sharing wisdom. "Listen. You have a good heart. That's why you're good at this. But don't take it home with you. Don't carry the whole system on your back."

Mara stared at her.

"I'm not carrying it," she said quietly. "I'm inside it."

Darlene's expression softened in something like sympathy.

"Exactly. So do your part. Don't do other people's parts. That's how you burn out." Then she walked away, shoes clicking, leaving Mara with the buzzing monitor and the green check mark glowing in Mateo's file. That night, Mara couldn't stop seeing Elena's face when she'd said thank you. Gratitude was not supposed to hurt. But it did. It bruised something in Mara she didn't know how to name.

* * *

The next week, Elena came back. Of course she did. The clinic had given her a thirty-day promise. Elena would not waste it. Mara recognized her immediately when she entered the waiting room. The jacket was the same. Her hair was twisted up again, though now frizzed from rain.

Mateo was with her, cheeks less red, eyes brighter. He carried a small toy car and rolled it along the floor as they waited in line. Elena looked up and saw Mara behind the desk. Her face lit in recognition. Relief again. Trust. Mara's stomach tightened. When Elena reached the window, she smiled.

"Hi," she said.

"I brought it." She held up a paper like a prize. Mara slid the window open.

"You got it notarized?" Elena nodded quickly.

"I went to the church on Elm. They did it for free." Her eyes shone with pride. "I did it." Mara took the paper and glanced at it. The affidavit was stamped and signed, official now. Elena had done exactly what the list demanded. She had solved the puzzle. Mara should have felt triumph. The satisfaction of closing a file properly, completing the narrative. Instead, her gaze snagged on a new note in the system, one that had appeared since last week.

FSN CASE OPENED.

HOME VISIT SCHEDULED.

Mara's fingers froze on the keyboard. Elena watched her face and her smile faltered.

"Is it... wrong?" she asked, fear sliding in.

"No," Mara said quickly, forcing her voice smooth. "No, it's good. This is what we needed." Elena exhaled.

"Okay," she said, relief returning. "Okay."

Mara scanned the affidavit into the system. The red flag disappeared. The green check mark remained, now more permanent:

ACTIVE.

Another notification popped up:

BILLING STATUS UPDATE.

RETROACTIVE CHARGES MAY APPLY.

Mara clicked it away. Elena leaned closer.

"They called me," she said, lowering her voice. "The... the support people. They said someone is coming to my house." Mara felt her pulse jump.

"A case manager," she said, trying to keep her tone neutral. "They help with resources." Elena nodded, but her eyes were wary.

"They asked me questions," she said. "Like... where I live. Who lives with me. If Mateo has his own bed." She gave a small, nervous laugh.

"He sleeps with me. We don't have—" She stopped herself, catching the words before they became dangerous. "Is that okay?"

Mara's mouth went dry. The training videos hadn't covered this moment: the moment when someone asked you if their life was allowed.

"It's... they ask everyone those questions," Mara said, which was not exactly true. They asked certain people those questions. People who had been routed and flagged and categorized. Elena's fingers tightened on her folder.

"I told them I'm okay," she said. "I told them I'm fine. We're fine." Her voice rose slightly, as if volume could make it real. "They said it's routine."

"It's routine," Mara repeated, and hated herself for it. Elena smiled again, thinner now.

"Thank you," she said, as if gratitude were habit. "You really helped us." Mateo rolled his toy car along the counter, making a soft vroom. He looked up at Mara and smiled shyly, as if she were a safe adult in his world now.

Something twisted in Mara. She wanted to reach through the Plexiglas and undo what she'd done. She wanted to pull Elena back from the net before it tightened. But the signature was already in the system. The referral already made. The case already opened. The home visit already scheduled. The machine was already moving. Mara handed Elena a copy of the updated registration.

"You're enrolled now," she said. "You can schedule visits, get prescriptions, everything." Elena's face relaxed, joy returning like light breaking through clouds.

"Oh," she whispered "Oh my God. Okay." She pressed the paper to her chest. "Okay. We're... we're in."

In, Mara thought, watching her. The word sounded like belonging. It also sounded like capture.

Elena gathered Mateo and turned away from the desk. As she walked toward the exit, she looked back once and waved, her smile wide. Mateo waved too, small hand fluttering. Mara lifted her own hand in return. Her fingers felt heavy. Elena left the clinic thinking she had been helped—thinking the system had finally opened a door, thinking her persistence had paid off. She stepped into the gray afternoon with a folder full of officialness and a child whose cough had eased, and for a moment she might have felt something like safety.

Mara sat behind the Plexiglas and watched the door close.

On her screen, Elena's file glowed with completion. Green check marks. Active status. Referrals. Notifications. A neat sequence of digital events that looked, from a distance, like care.

Mara stared at the line where her signature lived, timestamped and permanent. She thought of Elena's question—Is that okay?—and felt the answer lodge in her throat like something sharp.

No one in the waiting room could see it, but Mara's hands were trembling under the desk. She placed them flat on the laminate, as she always did, pretending calm, and called the next name.

SECURITY DEPOSIT

You wake before the alarm because the apartment has already stopped pretending it needs you.

In the dark, the radiator gives one last sympathetic clank—the kind you only get in an old triple-decker on the East Side, like a friend clearing their throat before saying goodbye. The air smells scrubbed raw—bleach, lemon, and whatever last night's desperation was. The windows are bare. The walls look indecent without your things to lean against. Even the light feels louder, bouncing off the empty floor and landing nowhere soft.

Move-out day is a small apocalypse. You make coffee in a kitchen that doesn't belong to you anymore and drink it standing because you packed the chair you always sat in. The mug tastes like dish soap because you washed it three times and still don't trust it. You check the clock. You check your phone. You check the clock again.

8:14. Inspection at nine. Keys at nine-thirty. New keys at noon—if the payment clears, if the office manager isn't in a mood to be cruel, if the universe wants to cosplay as fair.

You pace the rooms the way a dog circles before lying down, except you don't lie down. You don't stop.

There's an old habit to it: your eyes finding the things that might cost you. The nick on the baseboard you tried to touch up with a cotton swab and the wrong shade of white. The hairline crack in the

SECURITY DEPOSIT

bathroom tile that was there when you moved in but now looks like it grew, like something alive. The spot behind the toilet where the paint bubbles like skin after a burn. The kitchen drawer that never closed unless you lifted it and coaxed it, the hinge crooked on arrival—the sort of flaw that becomes yours by association.

Outside, the street is wet from last night's rain. Cars hiss past. Someone's dog barks at nothing, steady, insistent, like it's being paid.

You want to be paid too.

You want your deposit like you want oxygen. You have done the math so many times it has become a prayer: if you get it back, you can cover the overlap between leases, the movers, and the new place's "non-refundable administrative fee"—a fee for daring to exist. If you don't get it back, you'll juggle the credit card again. You'll borrow from future you, the version of you who will eventually get tired of being robbed with your own signature.

The sink shines. The stove is clean enough to cook guilt on. You kneel and run your fingertips along the edge of the bathtub, hunting for residue like a detective. Your knuckles smell like cleanser. The skin along your cuticles is split from weeks of cold and scrubbing.

You stand and your knees complain. Your body has become a ledger too: itemized aches, deductible sleep.

At 8:58, you hear the knock.

Not urgent. Not loud. A polite sound. The kind of knock that assumes you will answer.

You wipe your hands on your jeans anyway, as though you might be shaking hands with someone you respect. Your stomach tightens as you cross the living room. The floorboards creak in their familiar places. You've memorized their language, the way they confess under pressure.

You open the door.

He's there in a neat jacket that doesn't match the weather, holding a clipboard like a small shield. His hair is combed into a shape that suggests order is a moral value. He smiles as though the smile is part of the procedure.

"Morning," he says. "All set?"

You nod, because if you speak first you might say something with teeth.

He steps inside without asking, the way he always has. It's his building. His air. His hallway. You flatten yourself to make room—a bodily accommodation you've practiced in grocery aisles and elevators and workplaces: make less of yourself and you'll be less noticed. Be less noticed and you'll be safer.

He glances around the empty room, and for a second you see something like satisfaction flicker behind his eyes. An empty space is compliant. An empty space can't argue.

"Looks like you did a good job cleaning," he says, bright, like a compliment might be currency.

You wait. You know compliments are often the softening before the strike.

His pen clicks once. Crisp. Administrative.

"Alright," he says. "Standard move-out inspection. Just noting any damages beyond normal wear and tear. As per your lease."

As per your lease. As per your signature. As per the rules you agreed to when you needed a roof.

He begins in the living room, moving slowly, his gaze sliding over the walls as though reading invisible text. You follow because that's what you do—attend your own audit.

At the window he pauses.

"Blinds are missing," he says, still smiling.

"They were broken when I moved in," you say too quickly. You hear the edge in your own voice and you hate it, because edges get punished. "Half the slats were snapped. I have photos."

He looks at you the way adults look at children explaining monsters.

"I don't recall that," he says. "There were blinds. We provide blinds."

Your throat tightens. The sentence is simple, the way a door is simple when it's closed.

"I sent an email," you say. "The first week. About the blinds and the—"

He lifts the pen slightly. A gentle interruption. "We'll see what we have on file."

On file sits in the room like another person. An unseen authority. A god made of paperwork.

He makes a mark.

Your skin prickles. You stare at the motion of his hand, that small black line that will later become money you don't get.

He moves to the wall near the corner, where you once hung a cheap print with two nails and a prayer.

"Mounting holes," he says. "We'll have to patch and paint."

You swallow. "The lease said small nail holes are normal wear."

He smiles wider, like he's pleased you read. "Small nail holes, yes. These are... quite a few."

"Because the plaster was soft," you say, and you hear yourself protesting a reality he can't feel. "The first nail ripped out. I had to—"

"I understand," he says, and his tone is a warm cloth placed over your mouth. "But we'll assess."

The pen clicks again, a heartbeat you didn't consent to.

You force your hands open. You think about the new place. You think about the time. You think about how being right has never paid rent.

He proceeds to the hallway. He pauses at the baseboard.

"Hm," he says, as if tasting something.

You know the spot. You painted it twice. You used painter's tape and still bled over the edge. The color is close but not exact, like an apology that uses the wrong name.

"Scuffing," he says. "Chipping. That will need to be addressed."

"It was like that," you say, smaller than you want. "There was already—"

He turns his head toward you, patient. "It's difficult to verify what was there and what wasn't without documentation."

"I have documentation," you say. Too fast. Too sharp.

He holds his smile in place. "You mentioned photos."

"I do," you say. "Timestamped. Move-in day. The tile crack, the water stain in the closet ceiling, the baseboard was already—"

He nods slowly, the way someone nods at a story that won't change their mind. "Send them over, and we'll review."

The violence is in the we. The invisible committee. The faceless review. Your file entering a room you'll never be allowed into, handled with clean hands, then set aside.

In the bedroom, the carpet has been vacuumed into careful lines, as if neatness might be persuasive. Without your bed, the room is just a rectangle of light and shadow, a stage after the actor has left.

He kneels—actually kneels—near the corner, like a man praying.

He pinches the carpet and lifts it slightly.

"Staining," he says.

Your heart stutters. You lean in and see a faint discoloration near the edge, pale as a bruise under skin. The ghost of something you spilled months ago—tea, Ramen, maybe—so small you laughed, wiped it, told yourself it didn't matter.

Nothing is small now.

"I cleaned," you say. "I rented a machine. I have the receipt."

You hate yourself for the speed of it, for the way your voice becomes a folder. But you do have the receipt. You kept everything. You have an envelope labeled MOVE-OUT because you learned, painfully, that your memory is not admissible.

He makes another mark. "Our policy is professional cleaning after each tenant. We'll deduct accordingly."

"Even if I already did it?"

He meets your eyes. "It's standard."

Standard. The word is a fence. The word is a shrug wearing a suit.

In the kitchen everything gleams. The counters are wiped. The sink is empty. The fridge hums like it's still working for you.

He opens cabinets. He runs a finger along the inside of a drawer, then studies his fingertip as if expecting dirt to confess.

"Good," he says. Another compliment, another coin that doesn't spend.

Then he looks down.

The mark is near the threshold between kitchen and living room, right where the laminate meets the tile. You saw it this morning and scrubbed it until the skin on your palm felt thin. It didn't lift. Not entirely.

It isn't big. It isn't dramatic. But it has a shape.

A familiar outline, almost comical in its clarity: a tiny map, the small state you've lived in your whole life—the one everyone forgets exists until they need a beach weekend. Or maybe it isn't that. Maybe your brain is trying to make meaning out of a stain. But the silhouette is there: an odd hook, a small bulge, the shape that makes your stomach drop because it looks like home.

He tilts his head.

"Well," he says softly, as if he's discovered an artifact.

Heat rushes into your face.

"It's a spill," you say. "It's barely—I've been scrubbing. I can—"

He crouches, careful with his knees. He traces the edge of it with the tip of his pen—not touching, just hovering, like a priest blessing something.

"That's damage," he says, almost gentle. "Laminate staining. That will likely require replacement of the plank. Possibly more, depending on whether it's seeped."

"It hasn't," you say. You don't know how you know. You just need it to be true. "It's surface. It's from a candle. A drip. It was a tiny—"

"A candle?" he repeats, eyebrows lifting. "Candles are prohibited."

You hear the lease in your head like a voice-over: no open flames, no candles, no incense. Rules written by people who don't cook anything that smokes.

"It was in a glass," you say. "A jar candle. It tipped. I cleaned it right away."

He stands. The smile returns, and now it feels like a locked door with frosted glass—you can see light but not warmth.

"I see," he says. "Well, regardless, the flooring will need to be addressed. That's not normal wear and tear. That's negligence."

Negligence. The word lands on you like a hand pressing down.

"It was already warped," you say, and the sentence comes out desperate. You point, then stop yourself, because pointing is too much. "When I moved in, there were soft spots. By the fridge. I have photos of the—the bubbling."

He looks where you indicate, then back at you. His eyes are kind in the way a judge's eyes can be kind right before sentencing.

"Soft spots can develop," he says. "But the stain is here now."

You want to tell him the soft spot was there the first night you walked into this kitchen carrying a box labeled BOOKS, how the floor gave under your foot like a secret. You want to tell him about the bathroom fan that never worked, the window frame that leaked cold air in winter, the maintenance requests that vanished like smoke. You want to tell him you paid rent on time through all of it. On time even when your paycheck didn't arrive on time.

But photos are only proof of what existed. Not proof of what was promised. Not proof of what was ignored on purpose.

The pen makes another mark.

Your whole body reacts to the tiny sound. A flinch you can't control.

In the bathroom he taps the cabinet base.

"Water staining."

"That was there," you say, and your voice cracks. "The pipe leaked. I put a bucket. I told you. Maintenance came and—"

He nods. "Hard to determine."

He leans toward the tub, finger hovering near the dark line where caulk meets tile, a seam like a scar.

"Caulking. Mildew."

"I re-caulked," you say. "Last month."

"Still present," he says. "We'll likely need to redo."

We. We will take your money.

He checks boxes: closet, ceiling, smoke detector. The little things that become large when measured in dollars.

When he reaches the front door, he turns, as if remembering he's supposed to be human.

"Overall," he says, "not bad. But there are some deductions we'll have to make. We'll send you an itemized statement within the timeframe required by law."

Required by law. Another invisible room.

"How much?" you ask. Your voice is too quiet. You hate that too.

He smiles, apologetic. "We'll have to get estimates. The flooring is the big one. And the blinds. And the patching. Carpet cleaning. Standard turnover. It adds up."

Adds up. Like your rent did. Like your overtime did. Like the late fees you avoided by skipping groceries.

He flips his clipboard to a page you can't see and speaks in a tone you recognize from insurance and customer service calls, from every institution that has ever greeted you with I understand while taking something.

"As per the lease," he says, "security deposits are meant to cover damages beyond ordinary use. It's not punitive. It's simply—"

"It's my money," you interrupt before you can stop yourself.

The smile tightens. A small change, but you feel it in your bones.

"It's held in escrow," he corrects gently, like you've mispronounced a word. "Until the unit is returned in acceptable condition."

Acceptable. Whose acceptance counts is never in question.

He extends his hand.

"Thank you," he says, as if this has been pleasant.

Your fingers hesitate before you shake. His grip is dry, controlled. You feel like you've signed something without reading.

He leaves, and the door closes with a soft click that sounds like the final stamp on a document.

For a moment you stand still.

Then you exhale, shaky, and the apartment seems to tilt. Your knees feel weak, as if your body was holding itself upright by sheer will and the will has just been marked down.

You look at the stain again—the little shape near the threshold. It looks innocent. It looks almost like a joke. A tiny home. A tiny reminder that you belonged somewhere once, even if it was cramped and drafty and flawed.

Now it's evidence.

You sit on the floor because there is nowhere else to sit. The laminate is cold through your jeans. Your phone buzzes. An email from work. A reminder about an appointment at the new place. A text from the movers: *On our way.*

Life does not pause for your dignity.

You stand. You grab the envelope of receipts and the folder of photos—the ones you printed because you didn't trust digital anything, because you wanted something you could hold. The photos are slightly glossy, showing the apartment on move-in day: the cracked tile, the water stain, the baseboard chips, the warped laminate by the fridge. The timestamp sits in the corner, small and black: proof you were paying attention from the beginning.

But the photos don't show intent. They don't show neglect. They don't show the way your emails disappeared into silence. They don't show the way you learned to live around flaws because you were busy surviving.

At the new place, surrounded by unopened boxes, you can't settle. You keep seeing the landlord's pen. You keep hearing *as per the lease*. You keep seeing that tiny map-shape of home turned into a weapon.

At night you lie on a mattress on the floor because the bed frame hasn't been assembled yet. The ceiling is unfamiliar. Your body is exhausted, but your mind keeps doing math.

How much will he take? Half? Three-quarters? All?

A week after move-out, you draft an email: polite, firm, attaching photos, referencing your move-in checklist. You write *per our conversation* even though there was no conversation, only his procedure. You cite timestamps. You find a maintenance request number buried in your inbox and attach it like a talisman. You attach the receipt for the carpet cleaner rental.

You read the email ten times. You adjust commas. You soften language. You remove anything that sounds like anger because anger is always used against you.

You hover over *court*.

Your phone buzzes again. Work. Another meeting. Another reminder. Your brain is a browser with too many tabs open; everything lags.

You don't court it yet. You tell yourself you'll do it tonight.

Tonight becomes tomorrow. Tomorrow becomes next week.

The legal clinic's hours don't match yours. Small claims requires filing fees. You research it at midnight, eyes burning, reading statutes that feel written in a dialect meant to exclude you. You find strangers online saying, *Just take them to court!* as if court is a casual errand, like buying milk.

Exhaustion isn't dramatic. It doesn't arrive with fanfare. It's a slow siphon. It takes your outrage and turns it into something thin and manageable.

You tell yourself you'll fight if he takes everything. You'll fight if he's obscene.

You tell yourself you just need enough back to cover the overlap. You'll accept some deductions if they're reasonable. You are a reasonable person.

You hate how quickly you become willing to negotiate with theft.

Three weeks after move-out, a letter arrives.

The envelope is plain, your name typed neatly, the return address the landlord's office. The paper feels thick, official. Your pulse jumps as if your body has been trained to respond to institutional mail with fear.

You stand in the kitchen of your new place, under a light that hums faintly, and open the envelope with your fingernail because you can't find scissors.

Inside is an itemized statement.

It begins politely.

Dear Tenant, it says—your actual name printed there, but it still reads like a placeholder.

Please find below the itemization of deductions from your security deposit, in accordance with the terms of your lease and applicable law.

The language is clean. It makes the taking sound hygienic.

Blinds:

replacement.

Labor. Wall patching and paint: materials and labor. Carpet cleaning:

professional service. Flooring: replacement of laminate planks due to staining and prohibited candle use. Labor. Materials. Disposal fee.

There is even a line for administrative processing.

You stare at that one for a long time. Administrative processing: the fee for having your money turned into their money.

At the bottom is the original deposit amount. Then the deductions. Then the remainder.

The remainder is so small it looks like a typo.

Attached is a check.

It is insulting in its neatness. A tiny rectangle of paper with a number that would barely cover groceries, a number that would not cover even one day of missed work for a court date. A number that seems designed not just to save them money, but to teach you something: this is what you are worth when we are finished counting you.

You sit because your legs suddenly feel far away.

Your hands shake. You press your thumb against the raised ink. You imagine the moment someone printed it—the ease of subtraction, the casualness with which your deposit became a line item.

You think of the stain. You think of the word *negligence*.

You laugh once, sharp and humorless, and it turns into something like a cough.

You could fight this. You could send the email now, attach the photos, demand reconsideration. You could file. You could stand in a courtroom and explain to a stranger how a tiny stain shaped like home became an exhibit.

You could.

Your phone buzzes on the counter. Work again. Another meeting. Another thing that cannot wait.

You look around your new kitchen. Boxes still stacked by the wall. A dish already in the sink. A note on the fridge from yourself: Pay rent by Friday.

THE QUIET PARTS

Friday is close.

You feel the quiet violence of it: not a punch, not a scream, but steady pressure that makes you choose survival over justice. You feel the hallway-with-no-exits design of it. You can turn back, but you still have to pay the toll.

You open your banking app. You hover over *deposit check*.

Your thumb hesitates. You hate yourself in a precise way, like you hate the part of your body that flinches before you've decided to. But it isn't weakness you hate. You are not ashamed of being tired.

You are ashamed of needing.

Needing is the leash they hold without showing it.

You take a photo of the front of the check. You take a photo of the back. The app processes it, a spinning circle that feels like a judge thinking.

Approved.

The money appears as pending, like a small mercy that will still take a day to clear.

You stare at the number in your account. It looks almost pathetic there, a coin dropped into a cup.

You fold the itemized statement carefully and place it in a folder with the receipts, the photos, the move-in checklist. You keep it because you keep everything, because you have learned documentation is a kind of prayer. You keep it because some part of you still believes you might need it someday, in some future where you have enough time to be treated fairly.

In the meantime, rent is due.

You wash your hands at the sink and the water runs clear. Your skin is still cracked from cleaning. You dry your hands on a towel that smells like new apartment and old worry.

You close your eyes and see the stain again, that small familiar shape near the threshold, transformed into evidence.

SECURITY DEPOSIT

You open your eyes.

You go back to your life—overbooked and ongoing—carrying your dignity like a box you keep lifting even when it bruises your arms, because putting it down doesn't make it lighter.

BOUNDARY LINE

The first snow arrived the way rumors do in small towns—early, confident, already carrying an explanation.

By dusk, Ridge Road had been smoothed into a single pale field. Mailboxes became dark punctuation. Stone walls softened, their angles surrendered to the same white insistence. North Smithfield looked as though it had been built for winter: pines holding their breath, the old mill buildings down in Slatersville crouched like cooled brick from a long fire, the road curving between them with the tired grace of something used for centuries.

Ezra Hart watched from his kitchen window with a mug cooling between his hands. He'd been back in Rhode Island almost two years, long enough to learn the difference between *hi* and *how ya doin* when it came from certain mouths, long enough to understand that people here remembered ownership longer than they remembered weather.

The house had come with just over an acre, which sounded generous on paper and felt like a part-time job in real life. It had also come with Glenn Merrick.

Glenn lived on the adjoining lot in a squat cedar-shingled place that looked built to endure bad contractors and worse winters. Ezra had met him on the second day, when Ezra was still carrying boxes and the word *neighbor* still tasted like possibility.

Glenn had offered his name, then—after a pause that lasted a full second too long—offered a comment about the line.

"Runs right through those pines," Glenn had said, thumb cocked toward the tree line. "My father put a marker post in. Must still be there."

On the third day Ezra found the post: a weathered length of wood sunk near mountain laurel, its top painted red. The paint had faded to something bruised. It looked less like a marker than a warning.

Snow made the yard a blank page. The world made it easy to imagine no boundaries at all.

That illusion lasted until seven-thirty the next morning, when a plow truck arrived with a sound like a long throat clearing.

Ezra woke to the scrape and groan. Orange squares moved across his bedroom ceiling. He pulled on sweatpants, went to the front door, and watched Ronny—friend of a friend, local man with a local plow—back the truck down Ezra's narrow gravel drive.

At the bottom, Ridge Road met the driveway in a shallow T. The plow had no room for elegance. The snow had to go somewhere.

Ronny pushed a thick wedge toward the road and left a new berm along the side of the driveway—a low white wall that looked innocent until Ezra saw where it ended.

Not in Ezra's yard. Not cleanly. It pressed against the pines, against the place Glenn had pointed to with such certainty, as though the snow itself had chosen a side.

Ezra made coffee and let the house warm up. When he looked out again, Glenn was already outside, standing very still at the edge of his lot as though the berm had insulted him by existing.

Without looking toward Ezra's house, Glenn raised his phone and took a photograph.

Something in Ezra's neck went hot, the way it did when you realized you were being accused without being told the charges.

He told himself it was no big deal. It was a phrase Ezra had learned to carry since coming home; small enough to fit in your mouth, useful as a charm. *No big deal* was what you said when a waitress forgot your toast, when an uncle told a story that made your wife stiffen, when a stranger cut you off on 146 like you weren't really there.

No big deal was how you kept a day from becoming a war. Ezra pulled on boots and walked toward the pines with his hands out, palms visible, an old instinct from years of navigating strangers in crowded rooms. Friendly. Unarmed. A man approaching in peace.

"Morning," he called. Glenn looked up. His eyes were pale, the color of old glass.

"Morning," Glenn said.

"That plow guy," Ezra began, and heard the excuse forming too quickly. "He just pushes it where he can. I'll talk to him. It's no big deal."

Glenn's gaze went to the pile of snow, then back to Ezra.

"It adds up," Glenn said.

"It's snow," Ezra said, trying on a smile. "It melts." Glenn made a sound that might have been amusement if contempt hadn't been braided into it.

"Everything adds up," he said. "Especially what folks think they can do because they've got a receipt."

Ezra's smile died halfway.

"I'm not trying to do anything," Ezra said. Glenn didn't answer. He lifted his phone again and took another photograph —this time of the berm from a different angle, as if capturing proof it existed in three dimensions.

Ezra went back inside with a neat, irrational feeling that his lot line had shifted a few inches without his consent.

Over the next week, the snow did what snow always did: fell, piled, turned gray at the edges, sank into itself, melted and refroze into hidden slickness. Ronny came with the plow twice more. Ezra stood at the window each time, wanting to supervise, wanting to control the trajectory of every pushed inch.

He waved Ronny down on the second run, arms moving like a runway attendant.

Ronny stopped and rolled his window down.

"What?"

"Can you angle it the other way?" Ezra yelled back. "Toward the woods on my side."

Ronny leaned out, peering. Snow collected on his cap.

"Bro," Ronny said, "your woods on your side are his woods on his side. That's what I'm saying."

"Just—please," Ezra said, and hated the softness in it. Ronny cursed and shifted the blade angle a fraction. The berm formed again, but this time it sat more centered, less aggressive.

Ezra exhaled, relieved. Maybe it would be enough. Maybe Glenn would see the effort, the respect. He turned toward the house and froze. Glenn stood by the pines, holding his phone up. He'd been there the whole time, silent as the trees.

Glenn lowered the phone, then smiled—slowly, deliberately. It wasn't a friendly smile. It was the smile of someone watching a man struggle with a problem he had already decided was insoluble.

Two days later, Ezra found the first stakes. They were thin wooden markers set along the pines, each topped with a bright piece of orange plastic that looked official from a distance. Between two stakes, Glenn had tied a strip of twine—flimsy, performative, but enough to suggest a boundary had been agreed upon.

The old red-tipped post was still out there somewhere, buried now under snow. Glenn's markers asserted their own truth.

A day later, a sign appeared, facing Ezra's house as if it had been installed for him alone.

NO TRESPASSING

PRIVATE PROPERTY
VIOLATORS WILL BE PROSECUTED

The language was clean as a threat. Ezra stared at it from his porch until his hands went numb. He told himself it was no big deal.

That evening, he heard a small sharp crack. He was in the living room reading. Jelly—older now, patchy in places, still loud with love—was curled on the back of the couch, tail twitching in sleep. Wind scraped snow against the windows like fingernails. Ezra told himself the crack was a branch, or ice shifting on the roof.

Then he heard it again, closer. Certain. Ezra walked to the foyer and opened the front door. The porch light made a weak pool in the storm. Beyond it, the yard was darkness and moving white.

At first he saw nothing. Then he saw the front window beside the door: spider-webbed with a starburst crack, a hole the size of a fist gaping in the center. Glass glittered on the hardwood inside like spilled sugar.

A broken window belonged in a different kind of life. It belonged to neighborhoods with sirens. To stories with fists. Not to a quiet road where most nights the loudest thing was the yelping of a fox.

Among the shards lay a stone, smooth and dark, the kind you found by the Blackstone River if you looked. It fit in Ezra's palm like a clenched argument.

He held it and felt something in him draw inward, a knot being pulled smaller.

He called the police because that was what you did. Because he needed the ritual of it, the paper trail.

A cruiser arrived twenty minutes later, lights off, as if unwilling to announce itself to the night. The officer was young, cheeks raw from the cold. His name tag read CHARLES.

Officer Charles stepped inside, looked at the window, whistled softly.

"Looks like somebody threw a rock," he said.

"Yes," Ezra said, holding the stone up like proof. Charles took it with gloved fingers, examined it, and placed it in an evidence bag with a shrug so small it was almost invisible.

"You have any suspects?" Charles asked. Ezra hesitated. He thought of Glenn's phone. Glenn's stakes. Glenn's sign aimed like a finger.

"My neighbor," Ezra said carefully. "We've been having… issues." Charles nodded like he'd heard this sentence in a hundred variations.

"Property line stuff?" he asked.

"Yes," Ezra said, surprised.

"Always is," Charles said.

Outside, Charles shone his flashlight across the yard. The beam caught the stakes, the sign. He walked closer, boots crunching, and read it aloud.

"'Violators will be prosecuted.'" There was something in his tone—not endorsement, not disdain, but recognition. Respect for the language of authority.

He turned back to Ezra. "You been on his property?"

"No," Ezra said quickly. "No."

"You ever touch his markers?"

"What? No." Charles pointed the beam at the stake closest to the driveway.

"You know where the actual line is?"

"There's an old post," Ezra said. "Red paint. I saw it when I moved in."

Charles made a small acknowledging sound.

"I'd suggest you leave his stuff; alone," he said.

"I have," Ezra said, frustration leaking through. "I'm telling you, he's been documenting, he's… he put up that sign facing my house."

"He's allowed to put up a sign on his property," Charles said.

"And I'm allowed to have a window," Ezra snapped, then regretted the edge immediately.

Charles's face didn't change.

"We'll make a report," he said. "But without witnesses, it's hard."

"My window is broken," Ezra said. "That's evidence."

"It's evidence something happened," Charles said. "Not who did it."

Ezra felt the knot tighten further. He understood something he'd always known in theory: the law was not a blanket you could pull around yourself. It was a tool held by someone else, and the grip was not always offered.

Charles took a statement. He promised follow-up with the practiced vagueness that meant none would come. Before leaving, he paused at the porch edge and glanced toward the pines.

"If you and your neighbor have a dispute," he said, "best thing is to get it surveyed. Settles a lot."

Settles, Ezra thought, sounded like *buries*. After Charles left, Ezra taped plastic over the broken window the way you did before a storm. The tape crackled. The plastic billowed in the drafts, breathing like a thin lung. Jelly watched from the couch, eyes wide.

"It's okay," Ezra told the cat, though he wasn't sure who he was reassuring. The next day Ezra drove to Town Hall on School Street. The building smelled like old paper and new linoleum. Posters about snow-parking bans and recycling schedules curled at the edges. Ezra sat in a plastic chair and waited.

When he finally reached the counter, he explained the situation: property line, neighbor dispute, broken window. The clerk who was older, glasses on a chain, listened with a face that suggested she'd heard every possible version of human pettiness and had long ago stopped being surprised.

"You'll want a survey," she said without looking up from her screen.

"I was told that," Ezra said. "Is there anything the town can do? About—about a neighbor harassing—"

The clerk raised her eyes.

"Harassing is a legal term," she said. "We don't adjudicate property disputes here."

"So what do I do?" Ezra asked. She shrugged, a small lift of shoulders carrying years of bureaucracy.

"Hire a surveyor," she said. "Talk to an attorney if you need."

Ezra wanted to ask whether the town had maps, records, anything that might hold the past in place. Instead, she printed a parcel diagram with rectangles, numbers, meaning nothing without context, and slid it across the counter like a concession.

Ezra took it, thanked her, left. Driving home, he passed the mill again. The brick buildings looked serene beneath their snow caps. He thought of how ruin became luxury with enough investment and the right signatures. He wondered who decided that. Who got to reclaim the past and call it progress.

When he pulled into his driveway, Glenn was in the yard talking to someone. A second man stood near the stakes. He wore a bright orange vest and held a tripod. He adjusted a measuring device, sighting down the line like a rifleman.

Ezra's stomach dropped. He walked toward them. His boots sank into the snow. The cold bit his cheeks. Glenn turned as Ezra approached, mild as if this were a chance meeting at a farmer's market.

"Ezra," Glenn said. "Good timing."

"What's this?" Ezra asked, already knowing.

"Survey," Glenn said. "Figured we might as well settle it."

"I was going to do that," Ezra said, voice tight.

"You can," Glenn said. "But I got ahead of it. Saves time."

"You hired a surveyor," Ezra said slowly, "without telling me."

"It's my property," Glenn said.

"It involves my property," Ezra said. Glenn's eyes narrowed slightly. "Does it? We'll see."

The surveyor—William, according to the stitched name on his vest—

finally looked up. His face was neutral, trained not to absorb the drama around him.

"Gentlemen," William said, with the tired diplomacy of a man who made his living by watching people argue about invisible lines.

"What will you do?" Ezra heard himself ask.

William gestured to his equipment.

"Locate the boundary based on deeds and existing markers," he said. "If there's an iron pin, a stone bound, an old post… those help. If not, we establish from what's on file."

Ezra looked toward the pines. The old red-tipped post was buried somewhere under snow, hidden now. Glenn's stakes, bright, insisted on being seen.

"Can I see the deed you're using?" Ezra asked. William's eyes flicked to Glenn.

"It's public record. You can get your own copy," Glenn said. Ezra felt something shift—not heat, but something colder. Glenn had already framed this so Ezra would be the latecomer, the reactive man asking permission.

William returned to work. Glenn watched Ezra with quiet satisfaction.

"I didn't throw that rock," Glenn said suddenly. Ezra's eyes snapped to him.

"I didn't accuse you to your face," Ezra said.

"You called the police," Glenn said.

"How do you know that?" Ezra asked.

"Small town," Glenn said, as if that explained everything. Glenn looked past Ezra, toward Ezra's house where the plastic still covered the window. "You're new," Glenn said. "You don't understand how things work here."

"Explain it," Ezra said. Glenn leaned a fraction closer, voice lower.

"The law," Glenn said, "is a lever. It moves what it's meant to move."

"You saying it's meant to move me?" Ezra asked. Glenn smiled, but there was no pleasure in it. Only certainty.

"I'm saying," Glenn said, "it moves what it can." William called numbers to himself and wrote them down. The pencil scratched paper, the only honest sound.

Ezra went back inside and closed the door with more force than necessary. Jelly met him in the hallway, tail high, voice loud with complaint.

"Yeah," Ezra murmured, scratching the cat's head. "I know." Over the next week, things did not improve. They tightened.

Ezra found a long scratch along the side of his car one morning, deep enough to catch a fingernail. No note. No witness. The scratch ran like a sentence.

A day later, his trash barrel was knocked over, refuse scattered in the snow like a petty confession. Ezra picked it up in silence, hands numb, cheeks burning.

He tried to keep Jelly inside. Jelly hated it. The cat paced and yowled, tried to slip out when Ezra opened the door. Ezra became a bouncer in his own home, guarding the threshold.

On Thursday, Ezra opened the back door to bring in a package and Jelly shot past his legs like a streak.

"Jelly!" Ezra lunged too late. The cat dashed into the yard and disappeared toward the pines. Ezra shoved his feet into boots and followed, calling Jelly's name, voice sharp with fear.

He reached the tree line and stopped. William's work had concluded, and Glenn had replaced temporary markers with something more permanent: metal posts driven into the ground, each topped with an orange cap. Bright. Precise. He'd strung caution tape between two of them—yellow plastic fluttering in the wind, like a ribbon you didn't want to touch.

Ezra stared at it. He'd never seen caution tape used in a yard. It made the boundary look like a crime scene.

"Jelly!" Ezra called again. There was no answering. No chirp. No rustle. Only the whisper of wind through pine needles.

He saw tracks in the snow, small prints leading toward the boundary and then scattering. Another set, larger, crossed them briefly and vanished into the woods. Dog, maybe. Coyote. Or Ezra's imagination trying to give shape to dread.

He looked up and saw Glenn on his porch, watching.

"Did you see my cat?" Ezra called. Glenn didn't answer right away. He lifted his hand and pointed—not at the woods, but at the line.

Ezra felt his voice rise despite himself.

"You're telling me not to cross?"

"Not my rule," Glenn called back, calm as a man reciting a posted policy. "The line's the line."

Ezra could cross, of course. The posts were not a wall. The tape would break if he walked through it. He could push into the trees and keep calling.

But he saw, with sudden clarity, what would happen if he did. A photograph. A call. A report. Glenn's certainty like a blade. Ezra, new and already labeled as "the problem," would become the trespasser.

The law as lever. The lever already in Glenn's hands.

"Jelly," Ezra called again, softer now. The woods did not answer. He turned and went back to his house. His hands shook when he reached for the doorknob.

Inside, the rooms felt too large. The silence felt staged. He spent the afternoon moving from window to window, scanning the yard, listening. He set food outside, pulled it back in, put it out again. He made a small shelter from a plastic bin lined with a towel. He told himself Jelly would come home when he was hungry, when he was cold.

Night came early. The temperature dropped. The snow crusted.

Ezra stood on the porch with a flashlight, calling Jelly's name into the dark until his voice went hoarse. Across the line, Glenn's house was dark.

On Saturday morning, Ezra found a tree felled. It was one of the pines near the boundary. It was tall, old, thick enough that Ezra had once, foolishly, imagined hanging a swing from it in a brief fantasy of permanence. Now it lay on its side in the snow, branches splayed like broken ribs.

The cut at the base was clean. Fresh sawdust scattered over the white. Glenn stood nearby with a chainsaw at his feet, unplugged, as if he'd set it down only moments ago.

Ezra walked toward him without planning what he would say. He only felt the pull of it, like a tide.

"You cut that down," Ezra said. Glenn didn't deny it. He looked almost serene.

"It was over the line," Glenn said.

"It was a tree," Ezra said. "It's been there longer than either of us."

"So has the line," Glenn said.

"My cat is missing," Ezra said, and hated how pleading it sounded.

"I haven't seen it," Glenn said. Ezra looked down at the fallen trunk. Glenn had cut it so it fell away from Glenn's house and toward Ezra's side. The branches sprawled across the snow like a blocked path. A barrier made of nature. A statement.

"This is what you wanted," Ezra said quietly. Glenn tilted his head.

"I want what's mine." Ezra laughed once, humorless.

"Then why does it feel like you want what's not yours even more?" Glenn's mouth tightened.

"You don't belong here." The words landed with more force than the felled tree. Ezra felt something in him go still, not numb. Clear.

He understood, finally, that Glenn's war was not about snow or stakes or even property. It was about the quiet pleasure of deciding who was allowed to take up space.

"Okay," Ezra nodded. Glenn frowned, as if the lack of argument disappointed him. Ezra went inside and sat at the kitchen table. He opened his laptop and found a local attorney's website. He read words like *easement* and *encroachment* until they blurred. He filled out a contact form. He attached photographs: the stakes, the sign, the broken window, the tree.

When he hit send, the action felt both small and irrevocable. He understood this, too, was a lever. It would not lift him gently. It would strain. It would scrape. It would demand payment in money and time and attention. It would not feel like justice. It would feel like machinery.

In the afternoon he walked back out to the boundary. The orange-capped posts stood in a straight line now, precise and proud. Glenn had tied fresh caution tape between them—new, bright, fluttering.

Ezra reached out and touched one post. Cold metal. Unyielding. He looked at the woods beyond. He listened. No cat. No birds. The world held its breath in winter, conserving sound. Ezra stepped back. He did not cross the line.

He stood there a long time, letting the silence settle around him until it felt heavy enough to carry. He imagined Jelly finding shelter somewhere, curling beneath brush, waiting. He imagined him not waiting. He imagined the woods swallowing him the way it swallowed everything eventually.

The snow began again, light this time, as if the sky were shaking out the last crumbs.

Ezra watched flakes land on the fallen tree, softening its wounds, dressing it in white. Within a day the sawdust would be buried. Within a week the cut would look older. The landscape would accept the change without comment.

That was part of the cruelty: how easily the world absorbed harm.

How quickly it returned to ordinary.

He looked back at his house. The plastic over the broken window rippled faintly, catching light like skin.

Across the boundary, Glenn's curtains were open. Ezra could not see Glenn, but he felt him there, an unseen witness who had chosen absence as a weapon.

Ezra stood between his porch and the line, between his loss and the story the town would tell about it. He stood in a silence that was not peace—only the soundless aftermath of someone else's decision.

The boundary did not glow or hum or announce itself. It simply existed, as quiet as a rule no one remembered agreeing to.

Ezra turned and went inside, closing the door behind him. Outside, snow kept falling, making everything look clean.

CIVIL SERVANT

"What else do these places want from you?" she said. "You've got the diploma. Ten years! You keep jumping through hoops—what's next, a blood sample? Stool? It's their loss, baby."

He sat at the kitchen table with his hands folded, eyes fixed on the floor tiles. The grout lines ran straight and clean, intersecting at right angles, each one holding its place without question. He followed one with his eyes until it disappeared beneath his sneaker, pressing down lightly as if to keep it from shifting.

In the triple-decker's back hallway, the radiator knocked once, then fell quiet.

"You know, Ma—"

"It's all in who you know," she said. "You gotta be connected to the Mayor or the Pope, for Christ's sake. That's how it works now. It didn't used to be like this. You should be running these places. Hell, you should be the Mayor."

Her voice filled the room the way steam fills a bathroom—warm, wet, impossible to escape. She meant every word as encouragement. That was the trouble.

He shifted his foot and uncovered the crossing beneath him. The grout was nothing special—lime, cement, sand, water—but it held the floor together. Each tile depended on it, even the ones no one thanked.

His eyes followed the line to the table leg. That's when he noticed the envelope.

It sat beside the salt shaker, already slit open. A check, folded once, addressed to the cable company. His younger brother's name printed neatly in the corner.

"When did Tommy stop by?" he asked.

She paused just long enough to tell him the truth without saying it.

"You should call your uncle," she said instead. "He still knows that handsome weatherman. Maybe he could put in a word. With your degree and all."

He nodded. He always nodded. It was easier than explaining that he had already made the call. That he had followed up. That he had thanked people for their time.

The grout line ended beneath the refrigerator, sealed and finished.

He imagined himself explaining his situation to someone new—how long he'd been waiting, how qualified he was, how patient. He imagined the look of polite concern, the promise to "keep him in mind."

"I'll think about it," he said.

His mother smiled, relieved. Thinking was progress. Thinking meant movement.

She turned back to the sink. Water ran. Plates clinked.

He slid his foot forward again, covering the crossroads.

The floor held.

APPROVED GRAY

It had been close to nine months since Katie started staying with her father, Paul, in Georgia. When I called, I could hear him nearby—voice kept low, directed toward her. Then the swish of pants, the thump of boots. I pictured him upstairs in a closet, speaking into the sleeve-space between winter jackets.

"Why are you calling again, Isiah? She asked you for space... time."

Katie left after I asked for another baby. It was my birthday—the last time we had sex. She put her hands on me and said, "I'm your present." I treated it as a kind of answer. The next morning she was gone.

She didn't respond to calls or texts. The first time I called her father's house, he answered. From the beginning, Paul held a distance. After that, the language didn't change.

Space. Time.

I told him I'd quit drinking, joined AA, started grief counseling. He said he would pass it along at the appropriate time.

"Can you tell Katie I love her?" I said. "Can you tell her we can make it work?"

"She needs more space, Isiah," Paul said.

I drank from a Coca-Cola bottle half-filled with bourbon. During meetings I'd been using vodka because it carried less odor.

"She's in Georgia, Paul. Isn't that enough space?" I said.

After a couple of months he stopped picking up. Then one day—after

I rang for hours—he answered.

"It's over, Isiah."

"What's over?"

"The phone calls. The harassment."

"Put Katie on."

"Katie has moved on."

"Put her on the phone."

"Katie is eight weeks pregnant, Isiah. She can't handle this stress right now."

"Pregnant—what?"

I tried to do the math. It didn't resolve.

"You didn't think she would move on?" Paul said. "She told you it was over."

"Whose baby is it?" I said. "How—"

On the line there was breathing, uneven, as if the receiver had been set down nearby.

"Take care of yourself, Isiah."

I called again and again. No answer.

I finished the bourbon, grabbed my apron, and went to work. The store was close. Trees gave way to signage and the light of the lot. The home improvement center sat at the bottom of a hill.

A woman stepped out of an expensive SUV and walked toward the entrance with a paint-color fan deck open in her hand—another manufacturer. She spoke to the greeter before he could speak to her. The greeter pointed toward paint. My coworker clocked out ahead of me. Two customers were already approaching.

"Do you work here?" the woman asked.

She wore a tight white T-shirt, leather pants, knee-high furry boots. I wasn't clocked in. She asked again.

"Do you work here?"

"Yes," I said. I felt light-headed. I put a hand on the steel counter.

She waited.

"Can I help you?" I said.

"I'm trying to get this airy pastel color—9054 Approved Gray—in a paint that's good for my bathroom."

"I'd have to match it," I said.

"What do you mean, match it? I just want a pint or half-gallon. Can't you grab it off the shelf?"

I laughed. My vision doubled at the edges; I narrowed my eyes until she came back into one.

"I don't understand what's funny," she said.

"It's not one of our colors," I said. "But I can match it and mix it."

"I just want you to grab the Approved Gray."

I turned and looked down the aisle behind me—bases and sheens, cans waiting for tint.

"So you think I can just grab a can of Approved Gray from the shelf."

Her face tightened. "Is this your first day? Do you even know what you're doing? Get your manager."

"Everything starts white," I said. "We add colorant. There are thousands of swatches on that wall. We don't keep a can for each. There are multiple sheens and bases. Three manufacturers here. And you're asking for a brand we don't carry."

I kept explaining. I said something final. It stayed in the air.

A few minutes later, I punched the department manager in the face.

Hands grabbed me. The floor came up. My cheek hit damp concrete. A knee pinned my back. I exhaled and didn't correct myself.

When I came to, an officer tightened cuffs around my wrists. The manager stood nearby holding a paint rag to his nose. His "Excellence in Customer Service" pin was smeared with blood.

"You're going to get up slow and calm," the officer said.

The manager mentioned pressing charges and Human Resources.

"Not now," the officer said. "Give us a minute."

He shined a Maglite into my eyes, leaned in, sniffed twice, and angled his head away.

"How much have you had to drink today?"

"Human Resources," I said.

In the cruiser there wasn't much leg room. With my hands behind me, I turned sideways on the backseat.

The officer talked as we drove. At the Thurbers Avenue curve he pointed.

"Yesterday a family got killed right there. Tractor-trailer pushed a minivan off. Rolled a few times. Father got thrown out. When I got there, the baby wasn't breathing—still buckled in. Crazy scene."

At the station, a captain watched me through a narrow window in the door while he drank coffee.

Later the officer came in.

"We're heading to the ACI," he said. "Arraignment in the morning."

It was my fifth alcohol-related charge. I understood what that could mean.

"Do I get a phone call?" I asked.

"Not yet. Give it time."

At intake, a clerk behind bulletproof glass said my court appearance was delayed two days for the Martin Luther King Jr. holiday. I didn't have money for bail. After Katie left, the business went, then equipment, then savings.

They put me in a holding cell with five other men. A toilet in one corner, a phone in the other.

I picked up the receiver. A recording explained the rules and asked for the number.

It was late. Paul answered in a whisper.

"Hello? Hello?"

"Do you wish to accept a call from an inmate at the Rhode Island Adult Correctional Institution?" the recording asked.

Paul sighed and hung up. I tried again the next morning.

"If you care about Katie," he said, "about her future, about the future of her child—you will drop it now."

"Paul," I said. "Dad?"

He hung up.

I put my forehead to the concrete wall and held it there.

When I turned, an older man was watching me. Blue eyes. Nicotine-stained beard. White hair receding. Blue flannel. Paint-stained Dickies. Hands shaped by work.

"I'm just a little nosy," he said. "No harm."

"My father-in-law hung up," I said.

He nodded once.

A heavier man in pink cargo shorts was brought in next. He smelled like oil and vinegar. He laughed when he saw the older man.

"You again? What now?"

"I was just climbing down a ladder," the old man said. "Minding my own business."

"What'd you take?" I asked.

"Something I thought I deserved."

His name was Abner. He said he'd been an insurance lawyer. When we talked about family, he started to speak, then stopped.

The door buzzed three times. A correctional officer opened it and called Abner's name.

* * *

Two days after arraignment, they called mine. I followed an officer into a yellow room with desks. A bald man with a long red beard pushed a Ziploc bag across to me—keys, phone, Zippo, wedding band—with dried blood on the metal.

"Sign here. Initial here. Date it here."

Outside, the sky was starless. Orange lights washed the asphalt. Behind the fence, semis moved along Route 37.

A Subaru idled by the gate, sputtering. Sinatra played inside.

Abner rolled toward me and stopped.

"Come on," he said.

The backseat had been removed. Drop cloths and tools filled the space. A small aluminum step ladder was wedged between the front seats.

Abner sang along to the cassette. When Side One ended, he flipped it and whistled the opening of Side Two.

We crossed into Massachusetts and turned off near North Attleborough, away from the highway and into a trailer community in the woods. A brook ran along the dirt road. Rusted swing sets leaned in yards. We stopped at a drab double-wide with an Irish flag bracketed near the door.

"Come inside," Abner said. "Make yourself at home."

A lamp without a shade lit a corner. The place was packed with objects set aside.

A Darth Vader cardboard cutout stood near the door. Abner dragged it into the kitchenette.

"Took that from the cineplex," he said. "Worth a few bucks to the right guy."

On the opposite wall sat an undersized Wurlitzer electric piano with photographs stacked on top—Abner younger, smiling beside a woman with strawberry-blonde hair. In one photo a priest stood in the background and an infant lay cradled between them.

Abner brought five cans of beer still attached by plastic rings and tossed one at me. He turned on the TV until the picture emerged through static.

The Unforgiven with Audrey Hepburn was on.

"So," Abner said, "tell me more about the girl."

"She's my wife," I said. "Or was. I'm going to bring her back when I get down there."

"Down where?"

"Georgia. She's with her father."

I told him what Paul said about pregnancy. I drank the beer.

"If you want," Abner said, "I can drive you back to your place in the morning."

"I need to get ready for Georgia," I said.

Abner turned off the TV and picked up a bottle of whiskey from a stack of water-damaged newspapers.

"Follow me."

He brought me to a Rubbermaid shed. A combination lock clicked. Inside were paint cans—latex, oil, primers, sealers.

"I keep leftovers," he said. "Antique White for trim. Or I mix a bunch together and make gray. People like gray."

He handed me a flashlight and told me to grab towels.

We walked into the woods behind the trailer. Branches whipped my face. Abner moved with familiarity. Yellow tape marked a fallen tree where a path began.

"I'm eight days early," he said. "He won't mind."

The trees opened onto a lake. A canoe was tied near the pebbled shore. Dawn was breaking, reflected cleanly on the water.

"My son and I used to fish here," Abner said. "Perch. Crappie. We swam too. That water used to hit you hard and keep you awake all day."

He stared at the surface.

"The day after his funeral I joined a crew painting water towers," he said. "I needed to be elsewhere. I bought that trailer to be near this place. Every year on his birthday I come down here intending to swim, but I don't. I sit and wait for sunrise."

He wiped his mouth with the back of his hand.

"You mind if I paddle out for a few minutes before I bring you home?" he asked.

I nodded.

He pushed the canoe into the water.

I sat on the shore and tossed pebbles at an empty bourbon bottle. Only then did I register, without thinking it through, how Katie might have experienced me.

When I looked back, Abner had stood up in the canoe. He faced the sun with his hands in the pockets of his blue flannel.

In the white reflection on the lake's surface, I saw his small silhouette. And another one, just to his right.

His movement was slight—barely a shift—but I heard the splash.

For a moment, before he surfaced, the lake went still and threw back a hard, bright light.

Abner's body solved itself there, and mine kept filing appeals it didn't believe in.

CONGRATULATIONS

The balloons arrived early, which made them look guilty.

They bobbed above the reception desk in bright, unearned colors—pink, gold, a blue that tried hard not to be sky. Someone had tied them to the chair where Britney usually sat, so her swivel seat looked briefly abducted by a parade. Our office, for a breath, wandered into a better genre.

Jade appeared at my elbow with the speed of someone who lives for other people's milestones.

"We did balloons," she said, touching a ribbon like it might float away. "We did balloons, Harper."

"We did," I said. "They look… buoyant."

"That's literally the point." She glanced toward the conference room. "Cupcakes are in the kitchen. Alma's on the way. Victor's going to say a few words, Malcolm's going to say a few words, and Louis is filming."

"Of course Louis is filming," I said. Louis filmed everything; birthdays, fire drills, the time our copier made a noise like a dying walrus. He believed documentation was the same thing as love.

Jade leaned in.

"And we got the ones with the little feet."

"The cupcakes?"

"Yes. Little fondant feet. Like baby feet."

In the kitchen, the cupcakes sat in tight rows on folding tables, frosted in pale colors, each topped with tiny fondant ovals pressed into toe marks. Someone had set out a plastic tablecloth printed with storks carrying bundles. A Dunkin cup sweated by the sink, its lid clicking each time a cabinet shut.

Storks, I thought, have the eyes of assassins.

Sabrina was perched on the counter, immaculate, bored by her own perfection.

"Is it too much?" she asked.

"We can't be too much," Jade said. "It's a promotion and a baby!"

"It's not and," Sabrina corrected. "It's 'Congratulations on the promotion!' and 'Congratulations on the baby!' We are not legally allowed to combine them."

"Efficient joy," I said. "Lean celebration."

Jade laughed, relieved. The day was still clean.

In the conference room, a banner had been taped to the whiteboard: CONGRATULATIONS in glittering gold. Beneath it, sticky notes bloomed: You

earned it! So proud! Can't wait to meet the little one! Boss babe! (that one was definitely Sabrina).

There were none from Malcolm.

Malcolm was our director. He was polished calm, perfect suit, the sort of man who said family in meetings and meant loyalty.

Victor, Human Resources, was arranging chairs in a semicircle like we were about to hold hands and confess. He handed me paper plates printed with gold stars.

"Can you put these out?" he said. Then, quieter: "And can you make sure Alma feels…"

"Celebrated," I supplied, because that was the script.

Victor's fingers lingered on the plates an extra beat, as if he were trying to tell me something without using nouns. Then he moved on to the banner, smoothing it again.

Coworkers drifted in bright as confetti. Sabrina set up her ring light on the windowsill—"better lighting," she said. Louis did a slow pan of the room with his phone held horizontally.

"And here," he narrated softly, "we see the wild office herd preparing to honor one of its own."

"Stop," Ruth said, and smiled anyway.

Ruth was older than most of us. Her smile felt earned. She'd brought fruit skewers—grapes, melon, pineapple, strawberries—because Ruth always brought something that tried to be healthy in a room full of frosting. She set them down like a quiet argument.

Then the door opened.

Alma came in with her tote bag slung over one shoulder, coat still on, hair damp at the ends like she'd walked through indecision. She paused at the sight of the banner, the balloons, the semicircle of chairs.

A beat; muscle tightening.

Then Alma smiled.

We swarmed her with practiced glee, coworkers who had decided to be a chorus.

"Congratulations!" Jade shouted, and then everyone was shouting it too. The word bounced around the room, multiplying, landing on Alma's shoulders like a sash. Louis moved in close.

"Alma, say something for the video!"

Alma glanced at the lens. Something moved behind her expression, fast and thin. Then she adjusted, smiled wider, and looked straight into it.

"Hi," she said. "Wow. You guys—this is—thank you."

Someone handed her a plastic tiara that said MOM-TO-BE. Alma laughed and put it on because that's what you do when the room asks you to. She wasn't showing yet, not really. The party announced what her body hadn't.

"Speeches first, then cupcakes," Victor said while clapping his hands.

"Malcolm's going to start."

Malcolm entered with the timing of a man who believed the day would wait for him. He opened his arms at the room.

"This," he said, beaming, "is what I mean when I say we're not just a company. We're a family."

Ruth's smile tightened. I felt it in my own mouth like a sour note. Malcolm spoke smoothly, placing words like stepping-stones.

"Alma, congratulations. The promotion is well-deserved—commitment, agility, resilience. And the baby news! What a beautiful addition to the family."

Alma's smile held. Her hands were clasped in front of her, and her thumb rubbed the side of her index finger in a small repetitive motion, like she was erasing something invisible.

"We take care of our own," Malcolm finished.

Applause. The kind that sounds like one big animal.

Victor went next, holding a note card.

"Alma," he said, and his earnestness sharpened into worry, "you've been a stabilizing presence here. We see you. We're proud. Congratulations."

More applause. Alma's smile faltered for half a second at we see you, then snapped back.

Jade followed with a list of Alma's virtues as if reading a résumé to the universe. Alma's eyes flicked once to Malcolm, then back to the room.

We moved toward cupcakes. Louis filmed. Sabrina posed Alma under the ring light. Jade made her hold gift bags and pretend surprise again.

I watched the things the video wouldn't keep: the tension in Alma's shoulders; the way she angled away from Malcolm; the tiny corrections her body made when people pulled her closer than she wanted.

"Are you okay?" I asked in a brief pocket of space near Ruth's fruit skewers.

"Yeah," Alma said. "Just... a lot."

"A lot of little feet," I offered, smiling the right kind of smile.

Her laugh came out too loud, like a signal: I'm fine. See?

Malcolm appeared and her laugh cut off like a button press. He put a hand on her arm, just above the elbow. His fingers curved and stayed.

"You look radiant," he said. "Pregnancy suits you. Promotion suits you."

Alma swallowed.

"Thank you," she said automatically.

"Group photo!" Sabrina called.

We surged toward the banner. Alma was guided—gently, insistently—into the center. Malcolm's hand stayed on her arm until the last second, when it slid to her back for the photo.

"Say 'team!'" Louis shouted.

"Team!" we chorused, and it felt like a chant you're taught before you understand the cost.

When the flash went off, Alma blinked hard. Then she stepped away quickly, toward the hallway.

I followed.

The party noise softened into a muffled roar, like celebration underwater. Alma walked fast past the copy room, toward the unloved corner where the supply closet lived. She slipped inside.

It would have been easy to let her go. To take a cupcake. To keep the day bright.

Instead I knocked once.

"Alma?"

A pause.

"Harper."

I opened the door.

The closet smelled like paper and toner and cleaning wipes. Alma stood among shelves of printer paper, coat still on, tiara slightly crooked. Without an audience her face wasn't dramatic, just tired in a way that had depth.

"They keep saying congratulations," she said. "Like it's a spell."

"Promotion," I said, because I needed nouns. "And the baby."

"And the retention agreement," Alma said.

"The two-year thing?" I asked. "Pay back the bonus if you leave?"

"Yes. The bonus I haven't even gotten." Her voice went sharp. "And not just the bonus. The training. The classes. The 'investment.'"

My stomach sank.

"They paid for my night courses," she said. "Malcolm said the company believed in me. I said no, I didn't have the money. He said it wouldn't cost me anything."

"It did," I said.

"It does if I leave," Alma said. "It does if I don't… comply."

The word sat between us, sour.

"Comply with what?" I asked.

Alma took off the tiara slowly, like removing a prop.

"You've noticed how Malcolm is."

"I've noticed," I said.

She nodded once.

"He started calling after hours. 'Checking in.' 'Proud of you.' Then dinner. 'Leadership dinner.' Just us. He said it was for my development. For my exposure."

"And if you said no?"

"He heard 'no' as negotiation."

"And Victor?" I asked. "Does he know?"

"Victor knows enough," Alma said. "Enough to warn me in a hallway and then panic when I ask him to say it clearly."

Outside the closet someone shouted about cupcakes. Laughter. Brightness insisting on itself.

"And the baby?" I asked.

Alma's hand went to her abdomen—not tender, not protective. Just acknowledging.

"It wasn't planned. But Malcolm heard. I told Victor because I needed schedule adjustments for appointments. Next thing I know Malcolm is congratulating me in his office, talking about family. After that I know there's a party. There's a video. There's a clip where I look grateful."

Cold moved through me.

"He wants it on record," Alma said. "He wants me smiling while everyone watches. So if I'm unhappy later, if I say something later, everyone will remember this. They'll say, But you were fine. But we celebrated you."

"This party," I said, throat tight, "is part of the contract."

"It's part of the trap," Alma said.

Action rose in me like a reflex.

"We can go to HR. We can document. We can go above Victor."

"No," Alma said. "No, Harper."

"Because you think they won't believe you."

"Because they already have a story," she said. "And because he's not just him. He's the job. He's the insurance. He's the part of the building that decides whether I get to keep my life stable." She looked at the closet door as if it might be listening. "I just need to get through this," she said.

I wanted to argue her into safety. I wanted to hand her another world. Instead I nodded, because nodding was all the moment allowed.

"Okay," I said. "I'm here."

We stepped back into the hallway. Alma's smile returned before we reached the conference room door. Malcolm clapped his hands.

"Okay, everyone! One more thing. Team video. Alma says a few words, then we all congratulate her. This is for the internal newsletter."

CONGRATULATIONS

Internal newsletter: another record, another bright veil.

Alma froze for half a beat, then smiled again. Her smile looked heavier now, as if it had gained weight.

"No pressure," Malcolm said, making it a joke. "Just be yourself."

Alma's eyes flicked toward me, small and desperate. I stepped forward.

"Alma," I said gently, "do you want this filmed?"

The room paused the way a flock pauses when the wind shifts. Jade's smile dimmed. Sabrina lowered her phone. Louis blinked like he'd misheard. Malcolm's hand stayed on Alma's shoulder, fingers tightening just enough to show.

"I'm just asking," I said. "Because it can be a lot."

Jade laughed nervously.

"Harper. It's fine. It's just a little video."

"It's for the newsletter," Louis said flushed.

"And Alma's pregnant," Jade added, as if pregnancy meant you should accept whatever came with a ribbon. Alma's smile snapped back on.

"It's okay," she said quickly. "We can film it. I'm fine."

Malcolm's smile widened.

"See? Alma's fine." Then, as if to be kind, he added, "Harper, I appreciate your... sensitivity. Truly. But tonight—" He laughed lightly. "Not tonight."

The room exhaled, relieved.

Louis lifted the phone.

"Rolling in three, two—"

Alma looked straight into the lens.

"I just want to thank everyone," she said. "I'm grateful to be part of this team, this family. I'm excited for the future."

She paused. For a second her smile trembled, then steadied.

"Congratulations to me," Alma said lightly, and the room laughed because it sounded like a joke. Because it sounded bright.

"On three!" Louis called. "One, two, three!"

"Congratulations!" we shouted.

The word burst from us in a bright wave. Malcolm's hand returned to Alma's back, firm, guiding.

The video ended. Louis declared it perfect. The room relaxed into chatter again, proud of itself.

For a while no one looked at me directly. I became a small inconvenience in the atmosphere, a reminder the veil could tear. Jade cornered me near the cupcakes.

"What was that?" she hissed, smiling while she demanded it.

"I asked if she wanted to be filmed."

"Why would you ask that in front of everyone?"

"Because she looked uncomfortable."

"It's a party," Jade shook her head. "People get overwhelmed. You don't make it about something else." Her voice dropped. "Not tonight. Please."

She walked away, leaving me with frosting smell and my own pulse.

Ruth came beside me and bit into a grape thoughtfully.

"You did what you could," she said.

"It was nothing," I said. "It was a soft question. It was—"

"It was a crack," Ruth said. "Cracks matter."

Across the room Alma was still smiling, still receiving congratulations like a burden of flowers. Malcolm leaned close to her ear. Alma nodded, smile fixed. Her fingers rubbed thumb against index. Erase, erase, erase.

"I hate this," I whispered.

Ruth chewed, swallowed.

"Yes," she said. "That's the correct feeling."

The party thinned into its ending; sugar fatigue, polite departures, watches checked as if time had betrayed people. Louis packed up Sabrina's ring light. Sabrina posted. Malcolm shook hands, gave compliments like coupons. Victor lingered near the door, pale, his gaze sliding away when it met mine.

I found a plastic container someone had brought for leftovers. Without thinking, I gathered what was left—cupcakes, fruit skewers, half a tray of brownies—and snapped the lid shut.

An artifact, I thought.

Not the kind of proof that mattered, not legally. Not the mark of Malcolm's hand or Alma's fear. But proof the bright thing happened. Proof we ate sweetness while something harmful sat in plain sight.

In the hallway Alma stood near the elevators, tote on her shoulder, coat still on. Malcolm stood close, speaking quietly. Victor hovered a few steps away, like a man who wanted to intervene and didn't know how.

Alma's eyes met mine, flickered—question, apology—then dropped. Malcolm followed her gaze.

"Harper," he called warmly, "taking leftovers? Smart. No waste. That's the initiative we like."

I forced a small smile that didn't show teeth.

"Just cleaning up," I said.

Alma stepped into the elevator. Malcolm stepped in after her. The doors began to close.

Alma looked up once more, her smile returning automatically because the hallway still had eyes. She lifted a hand in a small wave, camera-ready even without a camera.

The doors shut.

The hallway fell quiet, as if the building had been holding its breath for the performance and now, finally, exhaled.

Ruth passed behind me, purse on her shoulder. She paused, looked at the container, then at my face.

"You're taking it home?" she asked.

"Yeah," I said, and it sounded like confession.

"Good," she said. "Don't let it disappear."

I walked toward the exit with leftovers pressed against my ribs. Outside the conference room the gold letters on the banner still shimmered: CONGRATULATIONS. Glitter had fallen onto the carpet; tiny bright flecks that would cling to shoes and travel. The celebration would follow us out, carried invisibly into the next rooms, the next days.

If someone asked tomorrow how it went, they'd say it was perfect. They'd say Alma looked so happy. They'd say the video came out great.

I stepped out into cold air, the city waiting in its ordinary gray. The container in my arms felt absurd and damning—sweet, bright remnants of a trap everyone had applauded.

And the word congratulations kept echoing in my head—bright at first, then darker each time it repeated—until it sounded less like a blessing and more like a verdict.

PERMISSION

Carter's mind was like his body—heavy, sluggish, slow to act. Yet there was nothing about him that read as a threat. He resembled an ox: strong, stupid, obedient.

The day Carter opened his law office, he felt as though his life was a success. It was a corner suite in a row of small retail spaces with apartments built on the second floor. A barber specializing in kids' haircuts, a pawn shop, and a button-sized Chinese restaurant occupied the three other units in the strip. Just above the entrance was a modest placard that read: Carter Bell. Personal Injury Trial Law. The office was one room with a cramped storage area in the rear. Carter made it work as a bedroom most nights, sleeping on a musty red futon against the back wall. It was his dream to have an enormous gilded statue of Lady Justice at the entrance to the parking lot. Still, his vision and his means were not nearly as balanced as Lady Justice's scales.

Carter was a youthful giant, carrying his huge mane of strawberry-blonde hair six and a half feet from the ground. He moved his immense limbs without purpose. His hands were enormous and covered with almost imperceptible stiff yellow hairs. They were calloused like rough-sawn shiplap and strong as vise-grips. Carter's head was square, his jaw angular—arresting like that of a wolf. Like a fat dog, he plopped himself down in front of the bay window each day and looked out onto the street.

A sleek new Mercedes approached the parking lot. In the back seat were two blondes wearing brightly colored tube tops. The man driving could only be described as an oily union of the words trust fund and fraternity. The vehicle came to a brief stop, and a young man got out and waved goodbye to his traveling party. Carter recognized him immediately.

"Gabe," he muttered behind his mustache.

The acquaintance had begun several years ago in the back of a small lecture hall at Roger Williams University. The two shared the same table and, eventually, a Coca-Cola bottle half-filled with spiced rum three times a week. By midterms, they realized they lived two blocks from one another. Soon it became an understood thing that they were friends.

Carter watched Gabe walk toward the office, but it seemed like hours passed before the door opened.

"Carter!" Gabe called out.

"Gabe."

"How the hell are you?"

"Oh, not bad—"

"Just got back from a night out in Boston," Gabe said, sitting on Carter's desk, "with two smoke-shows and this buddy of mine. Goddamn, they were hot!"

Gabe told his raunchy adventures, talking loud and quick, gesturing furiously, getting worked up over trivial details.

"You should've seen it, bro. It was out of control."

"Crazy," Carter answered, bewildered, trying to follow.

"So I said to him, 'Say that shit one more time and I'll gut you like a fish.' I almost killed the guy. I can't try to dance next to a girl without some asshole asking me if I want to buy a rose? I mean, this dude is trying to make me look like a punk because I won't spend twenty dollars on a wilted flower for some chick I'm trying to bang. Really?"

"Yeah," Carter said. "That's messed up."

"Oh—and we had an accident too," Gabe said, already on another track. "It was awful. This girl I was with was up on one of those platforms dancing when it collapsed. I thought she killed herself. She went down hard and tried to catch herself—wrist snapped, I swear—hand folded the wrong way. And the edge of the platform split and caught her leg, so there was blood everywhere. Faulty platform, I guess. But the music kept playing and the crowd kept dancing. You should have seen it."

Carter had a vague idea that Gabe had been stuck on some girl for a long time. He wondered how Gabe hadn't gone home with her, or why the injured girl wasn't in the back seat of the Mercedes that dropped him off. As sometimes happened, Gabe provided the explanation without Carter asking.

"I promised a couple of ladies I'd take them back to our hotel for an after-party," Gabe said. "It was insane."

No further explanation followed.

"You want to grab a drink?" Gabe said. "Take a walk down the street to that hellhole pub you like? You got nothing going on, right? Come on."

Carter went out the front door with him, and the two friends proceeded two blocks up Reservoir Avenue to McCarthy's. It was a shoebox of a place, set in a three-decker that occupied the corner of the block. Gabe swung open the front door and trudged forward to show his independence. Carter remained on the sidewalk, gazing stupidly at the blank green awning and wrought-iron bars on the windows, troubled and a little confused by his second visit of the day.

From the moment their glasses landed on the shellac-smothered bar top, Gabe waxed philosophical about half-truths of politics and the economy. It was impossible to say where he got any of his information. As soon as they started their second drinks, Gabe was speaking at the top of his voice, shaking his fists, exciting himself with his own noise. He spoke in stock phrases and clichés. They rolled off his tongue with incredible emphasis, appearing at every turn: "Another day, another dollar"; "separate the men from the boys"; "better the devil you know than the devil you don't"; "the handwriting is on the wall"; "pull the wool over your eyes." Carter listened, awestruck.

"Really, it's the women that are ruining the economy," Gabe shouted, banging the table with his fist until the snifter danced. "Uppity corporate bitches claiming sexual harassment for everything. They're evil."

"Yeah," Carter said. "That's it."

Suddenly, Gabe was calm again, forgetting his rant in an instant.

"Hey, man," he said, "I told that girl to come by and see you about her accident. She'll probably be in soon."

The following Monday morning, Carter looked over his appointment book. He resisted all things technology and felt as though the souls of men hung against computer screens. He began his week's work. The landlord asked Carter's help drafting a will. He had a tenuous grasp of how to put the documents together; however, he proceeded out of obligation to the old woman. He worked slowly, mechanically, twirling the pen between his fingers with the manual dexterity of a sloth. His head was empty of thought when the door opened.

"Hey, buddy," Gabe said. "Busy? I brought my friend here to see you about that platform accident."

"In a minute," Carter answered.

Gabe and the young woman sat on a plaid couch designated as the waiting area. They spoke in low tones. The girl looked around, noticing the side table with several outdated magazines, many of which had a stamp of ownership from the Cranston Public Library. Through the door at the back of the room, she could see tumbled blankets on the unmade futon. She thought the whole office exhaled a mingled odor of stale alcohol, tobacco, and chicken teriyaki.

Gabe told her about Carter.

"We've been friends since college," he explained, just above a whisper. "Carter's a good dude. Strong as hell. He could pick you up off the ground with one hand. Right? Look how big the bastard is."

They shook hands, Carter nodding his huge head with its great shock of strawberry strands. Sadie extended her left hand; her right wrist was wrapped in a flesh-colored brace, the Velcro edges slightly frayed.

She watched Carter curiously. Silence pooled. The breathing of three people in a small space made the air close and thick. When Carter finally settled himself, he motioned for his visitors. Gabe guided the young woman forward with a hand at the small of her back.

She was petite and unmistakably attractive. Her face was oval and pale, but it did not lack warmth. Her blue eyes were long and narrow, like the half-open eyes of a baby, and her lips and the lobes of her tiny ears held just enough plumpness. Across the bridge of her nose ran an adorable smattering of freckles. It was her hair, however, that brought gazes to a halt: heaps of blue-black locks, a royal crown of bands, dense and abundant. It was so heavy it tipped her head backward, thrusting her chin out just a little. It was a gorgeous pose, almost confiding.

"Well," Gabe said, "I have to go. Gotta get back to work. Take good care of her, Carter. I'll text you later, sweetheart."

They were alone.

Carter was embarrassed. Women disturbed and perplexed him. He did his best to avoid them, cherishing a suspicion of all things female—the perverse dislike of an overgrown boy.

Sadie was at ease.

She sat across from Carter and told him about her case, looking squarely into his face throughout. When she fell from the platform, she fractured her wrist and suffered a concussion. The cut on her shin was secondary.

Carter listened, nodding from time to time as she spoke. The sharpness of his distaste dulled.

He thought she was pretty.

"Well," Sadie said, "it was a pretty terrible night. How much do you think I might be entitled to?"

"Well," Carter answered, looking at the floor, "after an accident like yours, compensation for your medical treatment would be in play. Lost wages and other out-of-pocket losses would be included as damages too."

Carter leaned back, hands in his pockets, eyes wandering over the desk and floor. He assumed she didn't want to be rational with the club owner. He supposed she wanted to sue everyone with a name: the club, the manufacturer, the city—anyone who might be made to pay.

Then she sat forward.

"I just want to cover my costs," she said. "So what you're suggesting seems reasonable to me."

All at once, Carter grew obstinate—resolving, with all the strength of a crude and primitive man, to conquer the club owner instead, despite the weakness of liability and the limited extent of her injuries.

Altogether it was about two months' work. Sadie came once a week and spent about an hour in the chair across from him. During those weeks, Carter's awkwardness and suspicion vanished. The two became friendly. Carter even got to where he could work and talk to her at the same time—something he'd never done before.

Little by little, by almost imperceptible degrees, the thought of her occupied his mind from day to day and hour to hour. He thought about her constantly. At every instant he saw her ivory face, milk-blue eyes, out-thrust chin, and huge tiara of black hair. At night he lay awake for hours under woolen blankets on the red futon, tormented with her, exasperated at the delicate web he found himself entangled in. Desire in him awakened—sharp and brutal. It was resistless, untrained, something that could not be held on a leash even for an instant.

Every Thursday, Sadie arrived and took her place opposite him. While at work, Carter bent his large frame toward her. His hands brushed her fingers when he passed a pen or a cup of coffee. He could feel her breath on his forehead and eyelids, while the odor of her hair—sweet, heavy, debilitating—came to his nostrils. Carter drew a short, shallow breath. His jaw clamped like a vise.

Carter enjoyed his time with Sadie with a certain steady calm, happy that she was there. This poor Reservoir Avenue lawyer—ignorant and vulgar, with his Pabst Blue Ribbon taste, whose only relaxations were to eat, drink, and smoke—was living through his first romance. It was inexplicable. The long minutes he passed alone with her, silent except for the scrape of pen against paper and the tap of computer keys, in the foul atmosphere heavy with smoke and stale beer, had the excitement of a car crash.

He bungled the case considerably, but in the end he succeeded well enough. The retainer agreement he had her sign allowed him to settle without her consent, and that included signing the release on her behalf. An award was agreed upon after negotiations among the parties, their insurance companies, and attorneys. The money was nowhere near Carter's expectation, but it covered her expenses with a little to spare.

On the Thursday of their final meeting, just after Carter handed over the settlement check, she asked if he had anything to drink—to celebrate.

"Drink?" he asked.

She took a sharp breath, covered her lips with her fingers, and nodded.

Carter offered her a room temperature Narragansett, but she politely refused, asking instead if he had anything more substantial. He had an old bottle of vodka, which he hated. Sadie looked as if she expected him to mix it with something, but there was nothing—not even ice.

She agreed anyway.

He poured again and again until, more nervous than he had ever been, he babbled about Roger Williams Park Zoo and the Budlong Pool. All the while she listened and drank—drank and listened. Her cheeks burned bright red; her breathing shortened. When her chin dipped toward her chest, he took the glass away. She fell asleep quickly and, with a long sigh, sank back into the plaid sofa.

Carter straightened, walked around the desk, and lifted her. He placed her on the soiled futon in the back room and covered her with a jacket. Carter stood over her, eyes fixed on her face. For a long time he watched her as she lay there—unconscious, helpless, beautiful.

They were alone.

No one was coming.

The evil inside him was so close to the surface it leaped to life, shouting and clamoring.

Blindly, without knowing why, Carter fought against it, moved by an unreasoned instinct of resistance. From within, an alternate personality emerged. Another Carter Bell rose at the same time as the beast. Both were strong, with the massive crude strength of the man himself. The two engaged in a life-threatening wrestling match. It was the oldest battle—old as the world, wide as the Earth—the sudden leap of the animal, lips drawn, fangs bared, hideous and monstrous, and the simultaneous arousing of the tamer.

Dizzied and bewildered by a shock he had never known, Carter turned from Sadie, gazing around the room. The struggle was bitter. His teeth ground with a rasp; blood pounded in his ears; his face flushed crimson; his hands twisted together like knotting chains. The fury in him was the fury of a wild animal in the heat of high summer. He shook his huge head.

"No. No!"

Carter seemed to realize that if he yielded, he could never care for her again—could never get himself back. She wouldn't be the same to him, never so radiant, sweet, adorable. Her attraction would vanish in an instant. Across her pale forehead, under the shadow of her royal hair, he would see the smudge of filth, the footprint of the monster. He recoiled from it, using all his strength to deny it.

"No!"

He turned to her files as if seeking refuge. But the charm of her innocence and helplessness came over him again, a final protest against his resolve. He leaned over and kissed her full on the mouth. He slid his fingers under her belt and down her pelvis.

It was done before he knew it.

He was still trembling, still vibrating with the throes of the crisis, but he was the master. The animal was back in the cage—for now, at least.

The brute remained, awakened. Carter felt it tugging at its chain, shaking its cage, waiting. What was this vicious thing knitted to his flesh? Beneath the surface, his blood flowed with the hate and obscenity of his ancestors. His neurons fired with the transgressions of generations. To make sense of the opinions of dead men was beyond him.

Carter went for a cup of coffee. As he clunked back toward the futon, Sadie came back to herself with a long sigh. She still felt drunk and lay quietly.

Carter sipped his coffee.

"Ugh. I'm so sorry," Sadie said. "I didn't eat today, and I've been exhausted. I'm embarrassed. I hope I didn't put you out."

Carter turned to her, coffee in one hand, settlement check in the other.

"I love you," he said, with the unconscionable directness of an adolescent.

Sadie sat up quickly, then drew back, frightened and bewildered.

"I love you," he said again.

"What are you talking about?" she cried, suddenly aware of the positioning of her clothing. Her words were sandpaper on her tongue. Her thirst was unbearable, and her headache was so bad she could feel her pulse hammering inside her left eye. "What do you mean? What's going on?"

"I love you," Carter repeated.

"I need to—Are you crazy?" she blurted, seized with a fear of him—the intuitive fear of prey.

Carter kept saying the same thing.

"No, no," she cried, shaking her head, trying to get up and losing her balance. Carter came toward her, repeating the same three words.

"No," she cried, terrified.

As she tried to pick herself up off the floor, she vomited. It wasn't unusual after several shots of cheap vodka, but this expulsion was aided by dread. It startled Carter out of his stupor. He turned the handle of his coffee cup and held it to her lips.

"Here," he said. "Swallow this."

* * *

A week later, Carter lay on the floor in his boxers, doing nothing, gazing up at the ceiling, lost in thought. Since the young woman ran from his office, the panic of being arrested devoured him. After three or four days passed without incident, he took her silence as mercy. Whether from shock, shame, or simple self-preservation, she did not report him—she just vanished from his world. Now there was no going back. It was her, and no one else. Carter had to have her despite everything—had to have her even in spite of herself. Not once did he stop to think what that meant.

The following Sunday, Carter met Gabe at McCarthy's Pub.

"What do you have going on this afternoon, bro?" Gabe asked as they sipped cheap bourbon.

"Nothing," Carter replied, shaking his head. His mouth was full of bar pretzels. The bourbon warmed him, and beads of perspiration stood across the bridge of his nose. He looked forward to an afternoon of drinking and smoking cigarettes as usual.

"Hey, let's head over to the East Side, huh?" Gabe said. "Get some fresh air. Get the blood pumping, right? Maybe we can walk up College Hill or down Thayer Street. Hit up some bars."

They walked for upwards of three hours—along the length of Memorial Boulevard and across the Moshassuck and Woonasquatucket Rivers at Canal Street. Then they turned down North Main and halted at a few different stops for whiskey. Gabe kept swearing he wasn't drunk, only claiming his mouth was dry.

After trudging up College Hill and over to Thayer Street, the two pulled up stools at a dive college bar across from Brown. A mammoth old jukebox rattled out Bob Dylan's "Knockin' on Heaven's Door." From outside came the long, rhythmical rush of college students cackling and chasing things—their futures, shots, and ass.

Carter had been silent and preoccupied throughout the afternoon. Gabe noticed.

"What's the matter with you?" Gabe asked, slamming down his glass. "You got a beef or something? Spit it out, dude."

"No, no," Carter said, staring at the floor. "Nothing."

He held his silence. The jukebox slid into a new tune.

"I get it!" Gabe exclaimed with a short laugh. "This is about some chick."

Carter gasped and shuffled his enormous feet under the table.

"Well, something's got a hold of you," Gabe said. "C'mon—spit it out."

Carter began to feel that life was too much. How did it get to this point? A couple of months ago, he was content taking his small pleasures as he found them. His life had shaped itself; it would have continued along the same lines. Then this woman entered his small world and, instantly, the disturbing element appeared. Wherever she stepped, complications sprang up like the sudden growth of strange weeds.

"Carter," Gabe said, "spill it. You get some bitch knocked up?"

"No," Carter said, red-faced.

"Out with it."

The situation had gotten beyond him.

"It's—it's her," Carter said.

* * *

The days passed. Carter's shame and fear broke up little by little. He would never have Sadie, he saw that. She was too good for him—too gentle, too gracious, too beautifully made for someone so coarse, so enormous, so stupid. She was made for someone else. Sadie should have gone to some other lawyer—the young one down the street, for instance, the rider of Harleys, the gambler. Carter began to loathe and envy the man. He spied on him going in and out of his office and noted his salmon-pink neckties and Burberry plaid jackets.

Gabe told Carter about an event he was going to the following Friday. Sadie's cousin was hosting a fundraiser for the Future Female Leaders of Rhode Island Organization. It was being held in a middle school gymnasium in Providence. Gabe had somehow, as usual, found a way to get tickets.

Carter was furious at the thought of Sadie mingling with the Rhode

Island elite. He wanted Sadie all to himself. He wanted to take her—stopping at nothing, asking no questions—to have her, and by brute strength alone carry her away somewhere, he didn't know exactly where, to some small island, some undiscovered paradise where there were no Friday nights.

They didn't arrive at the fundraiser until last call. Carter immediately spotted Sadie speaking with two men on the opposite side of the gym. He tried to lie low while following Gabe to the wine station. The situation was awful. Carter couldn't rise to it. Sadie's presence was too much.

Who are those guys?

They were both after her, presumably, and now Carter knew he had to rush. There was nobody he would have preferred to tell his troubles to more than Sadie, and yet there she was—the mechanism of silence.

"I'm going to the bathroom," Carter said.

"Any more than one shake and you're playing with yourself, dude," Gabe said.

Carter lingered at the fringe of the crowd. He kept Sadie locked in his sight while trying to conceal his presence. As the crowd dwindled, Sadie excused herself from the men and walked toward a short flight of stairs near the entrance. Carter followed her down and paused while she entered the women's restroom. The fluorescent hallway lights buzzed with conviction.

He thrust open the door. The thud was thunderous.

"Hello?" Sadie called from behind a stall door.

In the stillness that followed, water dripped from the sink with the steady tick of a clock.

Then a ferocious blow swung the stall door open.

Carter stood over her. He was intoxicated, but not the kind that sways and wavers. He was watchful—vigilant, savage, cruel. In an instant, she knew—like a prophecy of the future shouldered by the present—what would come next.

Sadie dove to the floor and slid under the partition into the adjoining stall. She bolted the door and retreated to the back wall on top of the toilet tank, gasping and shaking.

Carter clutched the stall door with both hands. She watched with dread as his fingers curled over the top. The pinkish hue of his skin gave way to the whiteness of pressure.

"Carter, please," she cried, cowering, hands out in front of her. "Wait—please—stop!"

With a sharp metallic snap, the door was gone. His enormous frame stood before her like a monument to barbarism. She slunk down, imprisoned in his shadow.

"Please, Carter. No. Please. I'll scream!"

She shouted and screeched and bawled. The music was still playing and the people were still mingling. Her cries were stifled and suppressed. The noise reverberated enough to hurt her own ears, but it was only muffled noise to those above.

Carter grabbed her by the hair with his gigantic fist and dragged her from the stall. He tossed her to the ground in front of him, shoulders square, his back to the door.

"I love you," he said, pausing over her.

"Please, Carter. Let me go," Sadie cried.

"I've loved you every moment since I met you."

Blood pounded in his ears. He shook his huge head.

"No," she said.

"I do," Carter said. "I love you."

"No. No!" she cried, and then, with sudden determination: "NO!"

"You won't give this one simple thing to me?"

"No."

Sadie's reply roused the once slow and plodding man with the alertness and dexterity of a lion. He fixed his gaze on her, then drove his oversized foot into the center of her mouth. Her front teeth shattered and her tongue split. Blood gushed over her lips, suppressing her screams, muzzling her. She tried to fight back—kicking and clawing with the energy of something primordial. Sadie's intensity and resistance was so raw it piqued Carter's rage.

He took hold of her by the bangs with his left hand, eyes lit with primitive fire, and his sledgehammer of a right went to work—lost beneath the cookie-cutter pop song above, where the cracks and crunches, the gurgling and stifled thumps, blurred into noise.

In an instant—

Silence.

Then Carter came out of the restroom, walked up the stairs, and left Gabe standing at the wine station with a girl he had never seen before. The lights were up, signaling the end of the event. Carter walked out the front door without incident.

* * *

Just before morning, Sadie died. Her body gave up a few twitches and the occasional rattle before succumbing to her injuries. Her limbs spread in unnatural positions in a pool of her own blood. In her final seconds, a slow succession of wheezes signaled the winding down—like an old cassette tape warbling and unraveling into noiselessness. There she lay, cold and alone, until Monday morning.

The middle-school girls, whose first period included Phys Ed, always used the restroom next to their lockers before the teacher called attendance in the gymnasium above. At a quarter past eight, four twelve-year-old girls were changing into gym clothes when one paused.

"Ugh. What is that awful smell?"

The other girls lifted their faces and caught it too.

"Well, whatever it is, it's nasty," one said. "C'mon, though—I don't want to be late, and I need to use the mirror before class."

In unison, the girls slammed their lockers shut and ran into the bathroom.

MENDED

The clock had been silent long enough to become furniture.

It sat beside the bread box, its glass face dulled by a thousand rinses of morning light. When it worked, it gave the hour with soft authority—tick, tick, like a small throat clearing. When it stopped, we noticed for a day or two and then stopped noticing, as though time itself had learned to tiptoe through the house.

I carried it to the table because I needed something I could hold. Something with edges.

My mother watched me from her seat by the window, cardigan on despite the radiator's clank. The sunroom held her favorite chair and the stack of mail I kept not sorting. The door between rooms stuck more often than it didn't.

"What's that?" she asked.

"A clock," I said. "The one you used to keep by the bread."

She leaned forward carefully.

"Does it work?"

"Not yet."

"That's a shame," she said, mouth turning down, as though she were always tasting something faintly bitter.

The clock was heavier than it looked. I turned it over and found the seam in the back panel. Old Seth Thomas. Brass key. Small door to touch the pendulum. My grandfather brought it home from a yard sale the year I was born—like a gift meant for the house itself. He'd liked things that could be fixed. My mother liked things that didn't ask you to.

I laid out my tools on a dish towel and opened the back. The smell inside was metal and old oil, like a drawer that hasn't been opened in years. Gears sat in still, patient layers. Everything looked intact. The problem was probably small—dried lubricant, dust, a spring that had lost its courage.

Small problems were seductive. You could name them. You could solve them, and the solving would show on the surface of the world. My mother would still forget, the mail would still pile, but the clock would tick. Something would move forward because I had made it.

"Be careful," my mother said.

"I'm being careful."

She reached across the table and rested her hand on the wooden case. Her knuckles were thin and papery, mapped with blue veins. It still surprised me, sometimes, that she was still my mother under all that fragility, like a house that looks empty until you turn on a light.

"This was your father's," she said.

"It was Grandpa's," I corrected gently. "Dad kept it going."

"Oh," she said, blinking hard. Her face tightened—what she did when she hit a gap in the world and couldn't find a bridge.

I didn't want to make her feel wrong. I wanted to make her feel held. But the days were full of small inaccuracies, and I had become a person who couldn't stop trying to line everything up.

"I'm going to fix it," I said. "We'll have it again."

She nodded, reassured by the promise, not the details.

"Good girl," she said, and the phrase landed strangely on me now. It used to be a pat on the head. Now it felt like a verdict: she had always been the one who decided if I was good.

I took the clock apart in increments and set each piece on the towel with reverence, like a surgeon laying out organs. In the sunroom, light fell in dusty squares. The mail stack—an old Stop & Shop circular on top—sat where I could see it: credit card offers, a municipal tax notice, the pharmacy's receipt with its long list of not-covered items. Bureaucracy had moved into the house and it paid no rent.

"Do you remember when it used to chime?" I asked, because I was trying to tether her to something.

"Chime?" she said, pleased by the word.

"On the hour," I said. "A little ding-ding."

She laughed softly. "Like a bicycle."

"More like a church," I said.

"I don't like churches," she said, and then, as though remembering an old argument, added, "They always want something."

She wasn't wrong.

I found the place where old oil had turned to varnish and wiped it with alcohol, careful not to bend anything. The work was intimate in a way the rest of my life had stopped being. It required attention. It rewarded patience. My mother watched me like she was watching a magic trick that might go wrong.

"You're very smart," she said.

"That's generous," I said. "I watched a video."

Her brow furrowed.

"The internet is full of liars."

"True," I said. "But some of them are handy."

She laughed, and for a second it sounded like her—bright, quick, slightly wicked.

Then my phone rang.

It was on the counter by the sink, face down as if it had something to be ashamed of. My mother startled.

"Don't answer," she said. "It could be them."

"Them who?"

"The people," she whispered. "They keep calling."

The screen flashed a number I didn't recognize. The clock's gears gleamed under the light, exposed like a small heart. I didn't want to leave it. But if I didn't answer, there would be a voicemail, and if I didn't listen, there would be consequences. The house was full of consequences now.

I wiped my hands and picked up. A recorded voice: This is a call from CareSure regarding an important matter. Please hold for a representative.

I closed my eyes.

"Of course."

My mother watched me, tense.

"Is it him?" she asked.

"No," I said. "It's insurance."

On hold, a tinny piano loop played like a lullaby designed by committee. I put the phone on speaker and went back to the clock.

A woman clicked onto the line. "This is Marissa. May I have your member ID?"

I recited numbers from memory. My mouth had become good at numbers. She asked for my mother's date of birth. I looked at my mother—smiling faintly, as if at a party where she didn't know anyone—and gave it.

"There's an issue with the prior authorization," Marissa said. "The request was incomplete."

"What's missing?" I asked.

Faxed to the wrong department. Missing signature. Updated diagnostic code. The list arrived with the calm of weather.

My mother leaned in, whispering. "Tell her to stop."

"I am," I whispered back.

"Tell her you're fixing the clock."

I almost laughed. The clock was the least of it. The clock was the thing I could touch.

"Marissa," I said, "this medication is already late. The pharmacy is out, and now you're telling me you need another form?"

"I understand your frustration," she said, in the tone people use when they understand nothing but have been trained to sound like they do. "Until the prior authorization is completed, the claim will be denied."

Denied. A door slamming.

"You can contact your provider," she continued, "and request they resubmit with the correct code."

"My provider," I repeated. "Her neurologist has a three-month wait."

"Is there anything else I can assist you with today?"

I looked at my mother. She watched my face with concern, as if she could read the weather of me even when she couldn't name the day.

"No," I said. "That's all."

I ended the call and stood there, phone in hand, as if her keyboard might still be audible through the screen.

Then my phone buzzed: Medication back-ordered. No estimated date.

I stared at the words until they blurred.

My mother watched me. "What is it?"

"Nothing," I lied.

"It's something," she said, and then, with a sudden edge, "They're taking things from you."

It landed like truth. The world had been taking things from me in small, official ways: time, money, patience, dignity. It took and took, and then asked me to sign.

"It's fine," I said too loudly. "It's fine, Mom."

She flinched.

"Don't," she said quietly.

"Don't what?"

"Don't be mad," she said, voice cracking. "I'm trying."

Something in me broke—not with a single loud snap, but with the slow accumulation of strain finally turning into fracture.

"I know you're trying," I said, and my voice rose anyway. "But you keep asking me the same things. You keep telling me Dad is coming home. He's not coming home. You keep forgetting—"

My throat tightened. "You keep forgetting me."

Her mouth fell open. Tears gathered, quick and helpless.

"I'm sorry," she whispered. "I'm sorry, I'm sorry."

The shame hit me so hard my vision went white.

"I need a minute," I said, and pushed the sticky door open to the back porch.

The air outside was sharp. Snow patches lay on the grass like forgotten laundry. For a wild moment, I imagined walking away—down the steps, out the gate, down the street—until my phone died and my name became a sound someone else made into the air.

Then I imagined my mother alone, calling for me and hearing only the house answer. I imagined the visiting nurse arriving to a locked door. I imagined the kind of tragedy that gets condensed into a paragraph in the local paper.

I did not want to be a paragraph.

I cried with my forehead against the railing, quietly, as if volume could make it worse.

When I went back inside, my mother looked up at me like a question she didn't know how to ask.

"I'm sorry," I said.

She nodded. Her face settled, a little less panicked, a little more tired.

I went back to the clock, because it was either that or scream. I cleaned, adjusted, reassembled. Each tiny screw found its place. Control, in miniature.

I wound the spring. The key turned, then eased. I set the clock upright and nudged the pendulum.

Tick. Tick.

My mother's eyes widened.

"It's alive," she said, wonderlit.

"It's just working," I said.

She leaned closer.

"It's talking," she whispered. Then, mischievous: "It's saying you're the boss."

"I don't feel like the boss."

"You are," she insisted, and for a beat she sounded like herself—the woman who used to look at me with fierce certainty when I was afraid.

I wanted to let that be true. I wanted to believe the superstition I'd built: if the object works, maybe life will. But the mail stack sat there anyway, bold print demanding attention. There was always another way the world asked for proof that we deserved to stay afloat.

A knock came at the front door. Not a neighbor's tap, but a firm, official knock.

My mother stiffened. "Who is that?"

"It might be the mail carrier," I said, already knowing it wouldn't be.

A man stood on the porch with a clipboard.

"Town assessor's office. Updated measurements for the property record."

"Today?" I said.

"Yes, ma'am. We left notices."

Notices. The mail stack. The consequences.

"I can't," I said. "My mother—"

"It'll only take a few minutes," he said, and the phrase only a few minutes felt like a threat.

"Is it your father?" my mother called from behind me.

"No," I called back, and my voice cracked.

The assessor's face softened. "We can reschedule."

"Please," I said. "Yes."

He handed me a card.

"Call this number. We'll find a time that works."

A time that works. Time worked for everyone else—insurers and assessors and pharmacies and the calendar's neat boxes. Time did not work for the body in the sunroom slipping away in slow increments.

"Who was it?" my mother asked.

"Someone from the town," I said. "About taxes."

Her face tightened. "They always want something."

"I know," I said.

She looked toward the kitchen. "Is the clock still alive?"

"Yes," I said. "It's ticking."

"Good," she said, and her shoulders lowered slightly, as if the ticking gave her permission to rest.

I helped her to the kitchen because dinner had to happen. Soup heated. Crackers on a plate. My hands knew the routine; my heart lagged behind. The clock ticked from the counter. Every sound felt amplified: spoon against pot, radiator's clank, my mother's soft humming.

"What are you making?" she asked.

"Soup."

"Oh," she said, pleased. "I like soup."

She ate slowly, carefully. Her hand shook. I watched and felt the familiar ache: love braided with helplessness, tenderness braided with irritation.

The clock's hands moved. Not perfectly—when I checked my phone, it was already off by several minutes. The mechanism, revived, was still imperfect. It might never keep perfect time again.

When she finished, she leaned back and sighed. She looked toward the clock again, as if checking on a pet.

"It's nice," she said.

"What is?"

"The ticking," she said. "It makes it feel like… like we're not just sitting here."

I swallowed.

"We're not just sitting here," I said. "We're—"

I almost said surviving. I almost said living.

"We're here," I said.

She nodded, satisfied.

"Do you know what day it is?" she asked again.

"It's Saturday," I said, and she smiled.

"That means we can stay up late," she said, leaning forward. "Your father won't mind."

The old impulse to correct rose in me—reality as moral duty.

Instead, I looked at her: the way she held my father like a small lantern against the dark, the way she needed that lantern to feel safe.

"We can stay up late," I agreed.

She reached across the table and touched my wrist, fingers light as breath.

"You did good today," she said.

The clock ticked. The radiator clanked. Somewhere a pipe settled with a sigh.

Outside, night came on, indifferent and familiar.

The clock, revived, continued to be wrong. At eight-thirty, it chimed once—soft, slightly hoarse. My mother looked up, delighted.

"It's singing," she said.

"It's confused," I said, and regretted the word.

She smiled at it as if it were a child mispronouncing something endearing.

"Let it be confused," she said. "It's trying."

The phrase sat between us, simple and devastating. It's trying. As if that was the best any of us could do now.

I rested my hand over hers. Her pulse was faint but present. The clock ticked on, imperfect and relentless, and in its wrongness there was something almost merciful. Time was moving, but not on anyone's schedule—not on the insurer's, not on the town's, not on mine.

My mother squeezed my hand once, a small anchor. In the dim kitchen light, with the repaired clock insisting on its shaky rhythm, we sat together—not redeemed, not saved, not fixed—just held for a moment by the sound of something still working, even when it didn't know exactly what it was doing.

SPITTING DISTANCE

Allison waited in the lobby of the Cineplex for the 1:40 show to let out. She wore the blue skirt Zachary had liked, not because it mattered to anyone else, but because it made the day feel less unmoored.

Outside, the parking lot shone with old salt and slush that never quite dried.

Two teenagers drifted past. One of them looked her up and down and said, "Well hey there, sexy." The other saw her face and offered something like an apology he didn't know how to deliver.

"Have a good day, he said."

When they left, Allison released a breath she didn't realize she'd been holding. It hurt to be watched.

Behind the concessions counter, a boy with a backward hat called out, "Good deals on snacks during afternoon movies."

She bought a large popcorn—"only a quarter more"—because standing in a movie theater lobby without anything in her hands felt like loitering, like being the wrong kind of person. Allison did what was expected of her so she could pass unnoticed.

The crowd emptied out in a patient line. Families in puffy coats, couples with paper cups, a few older men who walked as if their joints negotiated each step. Allison waited for the last of them and then handed her ticket to the usher.

This was her wedding anniversary.

She had tried to stay home. She had tried to do what people recommended—call her brother, take a walk, read, distract herself. All the small, sensible suggestions that assumed grief was a problem of time management.

But Spitting Distance was still playing here, over a hundred miles from her house, and the coincidence felt like a crack in reality. For a few weeks, Zachary remained in the world in a way she could point to. Not as a memory—memories bent under pressure—but as a moving body among strangers.

The box office run would end soon. Then he would be sealed away into formats and platforms, reduced to a thing she controlled. That wasn't what she wanted.

She didn't want to possess him.

She wanted to be near him.

Inside the theater, a yawning employee swept kernels and straw wrappers into a dustpan. Allison paused at the aisle as if she might leave. The shift in direction made her stomach pitch.

For seven years, Zachary had been the one who moved first. He made introductions. He chatted with cashiers. He filled the air where Allison usually went quiet. Without him, every public place felt like an audition she hadn't prepared for.

She sat. She did not look around. The audience was small, but even a small audience felt like an accusation. The world's laughter sounded obscene.

The movie began.

It was a bad comedy. Two college buddies bumbling across the country in search of something they insisted was love. Allison hated it immediately. Hated the easy noise of it. Hated the way strangers relaxed into it, as if nothing could ever happen to them.

Zachary's moment didn't come until fifty-two minutes in. He wasn't a character. He was background—captured by chance during filming, preserved because some editor decided the tiny authenticity was worth keeping.

That was the miracle: not that he was there, but that the world hadn't scrubbed him out.

She braced as the scene approached the sidewalk. Two actors argued while people passed behind them. Allison's fingernails dug into the armrests.

A woman with a baby appeared at the edge of the frame. The baby's tiny shoe was loose.

Then Zachary walked into view.

His gait was unmistakable. Not dramatic, not "cinematic." Just his body moving the way it always had, as if he belonged on any street, in any crowd, without needing to announce himself.

He noticed the baby's shoe and stepped closer. He spoke to the child. Allison couldn't hear the words, but she knew the tone. Warm. Patient. The tone he used with anxious dogs, with nervous waiters, with Allison when her mind began to spin.

He knelt. He adjusted the little shoe, secured it gently. The mother never noticed; she stayed on her phone, floating through the world.

Zachary did not mind.

He made a silly face at the baby—peek-a-boo, something quick and soft—and began to walk away. The baby cried at his absence, and Zachary turned back once more, made another face, and then—just before leaving the frame—looked over his shoulder and smiled.

Then he was gone.

Allison always stayed in her seat for a minute after, as if standing too soon would break the spell. She didn't possess the moment. That was why she came back again and again. Repetition was the only form of touch left to her.

When the movie ended, she rose and left without meeting anyone's eyes. In the lobby, her brother waited.

He looked tired, like he'd been living on the edge of her grief for weeks.

"Oh, Allison," he said. "I thought you weren't going to do this anymore."

"How did you know?" she asked, though she already knew the answer.

"I went to your house," he said. "You weren't there. I Googled showtimes."

She didn't argue. She didn't have the strength.

For two weeks she stayed with him and his wife. They spoke about hope in careful tones. They suggested hobbies. They made dinner. They treated her like something fragile that might break if touched wrong.

The more they tried to help, the more alone she felt. They meant well, but their kindness couldn't reach the place Zachary had occupied. It was like they were speaking through glass.

So she did what she'd promised she wouldn't do.

She searched again.

She found an old theater nearly two hundred miles away—second-run movies, bargain tickets, one final showtime: 9:40 p.m.

She left immediately. Panic drove her, not because she believed she could save him, but because she couldn't tolerate the idea of missing him.

When she arrived, the animated confections had already danced across the screen. She was late. She had never been late. She sat farther back than usual, furious at the small betrayal of timing.

A man with two children dropped into the seats beside her. He smiled at Allison as if proximity were a shared agreement.

Allison stared straight ahead.

The little girl kept glancing at her. She looked too young to be out this late. She yawned repeatedly. Her head began to bob.

Allison's body tightened with annoyance. This was supposed to be her last time. Her last clean run through the miracle.

As the sidewalk scene approached, the girl's head tipped sideways, landing awkwardly between the seats. The child did not wake, but her neck bent at an angle that made Allison wince despite herself.

Then the screen flickered.

A harsh whirr. A skip. The image scrambled. A blue flash. The scene jumped off-center. The audience groaned and laughed.

"Oh, come on!"

"It was awful anyway!"

"Someone's getting fired!"

Allison's throat closed. She leaned forward as if she could force the projector back into alignment with her need.

"No," she whispered. "No—"

The picture steadied for a second—Zachary visible, bent over the baby's shoe—and then jittered again. The crowd kept cackling, treating her private apocalypse as a technical inconvenience.

Then the image froze.

It froze on Zachary's face—on that brief over-the-shoulder smile—held there longer than it ever had before, as if time had decided to stop cooperating with the movie and, by accident, offered Allison a mercy.

In that suspended moment, she saw what she had been doing.

And Zachary, of course, had been doing the opposite.

He had moved toward the child. Toward the small need. Toward the thing no one else had bothered to notice.

Allison shifted.

Slowly, carefully, she slid her shoulder under the sleeping girl's head and lifted it enough so the child's neck straightened. The girl exhaled and settled. She didn't wake, but her face eased, as if comfort had arrived without explanation.

The projector clicked. The movie resumed. Zachary's smile vanished as the scene continued, and he walked out of frame as he always did.

Allison stayed still, supporting the child's head, her body held in a posture that was suddenly familiar. Not because she'd done it before, but because Zachary had.

The rest of the movie played. People laughed. People shifted in their seats. The father beside her didn't notice what she'd done.

Allison did not need him to.

When the credits rolled, she didn't rush to leave. She waited until the child stirred and sat upright on her own. Only then did Allison stand.

Outside, the night air felt sharper than it had on her way in. She walked to her car alone, but the solitude didn't feel like punishment.

It felt, for the first time in months, like something she might survive.

DROWNING CARNATIONS

The chaos of thought bludgeoned Maggie's senses as she emptied her third cup. Through the front windows she watched the brunch crowd come and go along downtown Providence—families in wool coats and polished shoes, moving in thick, purposeful waves past the stone and steel of a city that had learned to look sturdy in winter. It was a raw, oppressive season—two years since Maggie heard the broadcast about Hitler's death, since the papers ran the image and then turned the page. The façades downtown—banks, office buildings, glass-fronted lobbies—held their postwar confidence like a fixed expression. People held firm their hats, stared down their breath, and met themselves in the reflections. The reflections did not move. Nothing bloomed beneath.

From a small table by the window, Maggie felt the warmth drain from her freckled cheeks. She searched the dining room for the waitress and found her slipping behind the swinging kitchen doors. Maggie lifted her empty teacup, then lowered it again when no one looked. She nudged her tortoiseshell frames up the bridge of her nose and pushed strawberry-blonde frizz from her forehead. The cup stayed empty. Her composure narrowed to a thin, shaky line.

Agnes—four years old, untroubled—folded a clean white napkin into something that pleased her. The clink of cutlery amused her. She hummed to herself. Agnes had her father's face. Maggie found no consolation in it; it made the room feel more crowded.

From here Maggie could see the stairs to the second floor. The hostess stood at the base, smiling mechanically, holding up fingers to signal available seating, then dropping her hand when the message landed. The motion repeated with the clean certainty of routine.

A sharp exchange near the kitchen cut through the room.

"We're all outta champagne," a young man in white said—busboy, she assumed.

"Then don't offer it," a waitress snapped.

Maggie felt the words lodge somewhere deep, like a rule spoken too late.

When her own waitress appeared, she stared at Maggie's cup as if it were evidence.

"Another?" she asked.

"Yes," Maggie said. "Go get it."

"Have you decided on anything to eat?"

"My daughter will have the chopped egg salad sandwich, and I'll—"

"Noooo," Agnes whined. "I don't want egg samwidges."

"Sandwich," Maggie corrected. "Sand—wich. What do you want, then?"

"Banana split!"

Maggie pressed her left palm to her right temple and dipped her forehead toward the table, a small private bow to endurance. For six months she had saved for this retreat. Agnes spent most of her time with her grandmother now. Maggie worked. That was the shape of things. She could not remember when food had become a negotiation.

"Give us a few more minutes," Maggie said.

Agnes giggled behind her hand. She returned to the napkin, fashioning a doll whose spine was a teaspoon. Her shoes didn't quite reach the floor when she swung her legs; the chair gave a soft, periodic scrape.

"Mommy, you gonna have anothuh cuppuh grasshoppers? Eww." She giggled again, pleased with herself.

"I'll be right back with your grasshop—I mean tea," the waitress said, smirking.

Maggie watched her walk away—young, light-footed, unburdened—and imagined her own work clothes sprinkled with champagne and soft cheeses instead of their usual spatter of entrails and crimson juices.

Each morning, the waitresses lined up for inspection. Two stories above the street, the owner's son fussed over every detail: pressed black uniforms, starched ivory collars, small aprons like punctuation. Most of the women were Irish, "right off the boat," the phrase the cocktail crowd used when they wanted to sound amused instead of cruel. Those who failed inspection were sent home without pay. Maggie knew what that meant: long walks, no wages, no room for error.

She clung to her unfilled cup and wondered what the waitress's name was. It was never offered. There were no name tags. Names were for people who could afford to be seen as singular.

"Mommy?" Agnes said.

Maggie closed her eyes as if caught in a fixed blink. She took a long breath, lifted her glasses, and turned sluggishly.

"What is it, Agnes?"

"Did Daddy eva go to matinee?"

"Matinee," Maggie said, careful with the syllables. "No. Daddy never went to a matinee."

Agnes nodded, unconvinced.

"I think Donald Duck is a silly willy."

Maggie stared at her, throat tightening around the familiar softness of the face.

"I said no," Maggie told her. "Now we're not doing this all day. You're getting a hamburger. You will eat a hamburger. Do you understand?"

Agnes's father had been the center of Maggie's world before the war.

She had accepted his proposal before he could finish the question. The last time she saw him clearly in her mind, he was laughing in their kitchen, sleeves rolled, hands clean. Agnes was growing in Maggie's belly when he slept his first night east of the Belgian–German border, using bloodless hands to dig a shallow trench in the frozen Hürtgen Forest soil. Maggie had believed he could do nothing short of walking on water.

Not all deities returned.

The waitress returned and attempted to set down a teacup filled with crème de menthe, but Maggie snatched it mid-motion. The waitress's displeasure was contained behind a crooked smile.

"Have we decided?"

"Yes," Maggie said. "I'll have the Chicken à la King, and my daughter will have a hamburger."

"Noooooooo!" Agnes burst out. "I don't wanna hambrrrger!"

"Dammit, Agnes." Maggie's voice cracked. "You will eat the goddamned hamburger—or no matinee. Do you understand? That's it."

The waitress stood still. Her scrutiny sharpened into something practiced.

After Agnes's birth, Maggie had been charged with stealing an apple from a pushcart on Westminster Street. She had told the policeman she had no money, her baby was starving, and she was deprived of sustenance. The merchant wouldn't drop the charges. The prosecutor aimed for thirty days in jail and a fifteen-dollar fine. Maggie's mother paid double to avoid jail time and offered her a corner of a pocket-sized apartment. In exchange, Maggie took her mother's shifts at the neighborhood butcher shop, mopping trim-offs and shoveling sawdust onto blood pools. There were few positions for women from their neighborhood. Maggie could not refuse.

"Perhaps another few minutes," the waitress said.

Maggie fixed her gaze on the carpet and kept her teeth pressed together when she spoke.

"I will have the goddamned Chicken à la King. She will have a hamburger. Do you understand? Now bring me another one and put it in a teacup again."

"But you haven't even finished this one. Besides, we're all out of the crème de menthe for your grasshoppers. That's the last of it."

"What do you mean you're all out?"

"I mean we have no more. The bartender tossed the empty bottle."

"Then why did you offer it?" Maggie looked up at the waitress's ruddy cheeks. Her hands trembled upward, palms open, as if presenting evidence. "Don't offer it if you know it will run out. You don't get to offer something and take it back."

The waitress's face softened into the expression service required.

"Please keep your voice down, ma'am. I'm sorry. I'm not trying to upset you. We just don't have it." She glanced past Maggie—one quick check toward the hostess, toward the stairs, toward whatever counted as authority in this room. Then she returned her eyes to Maggie. "That's policy. There's nothing I can do about that. I can get you something else."

Maggie heard *policy* the way she heard *no*. She felt the sentence become a door.

"I was offered a life once," she said, and her voice steadied into a rehearsed recital. "I said yes in a cold church. I waved from the shore like everyone else. Carnations in hand. I smiled. I watched them fall into the water and drown." Her breath caught. "And now I pull the covers over my daughter alone every night."

She swallowed and tried again, as if a second attempt might be recognized.

"Hundreds of times."

The waitress did not move.

"No more drowning carnations," Maggie said. "Get me another cup. Go get me another. Get it."

"I'm sorry," the waitress said again, quieter. "We just don't have it."

Maggie leaned forward, as if proximity could rewrite inventory.

"You fill the cup," she said. "I empty the cup. That is the order of things." Her hands shook above the table. "You don't get to take my cup away. Not again." She heard her own voice rising and could not lower it. "You're not the judge and jury. You're not the gatekeeper."

Her words kept trying to make the room into a tribunal and the shortage into a verdict.

"The gate is blown to hell," Maggie said, voice breaking, "and I will not be denied."

As Maggie flared, her glasses slid down her nose, struck Agnes's napkin doll, and dropped somewhere under the table. The brassy murmuring of the brunch crowd stopped. Judgment arrived all at once—every eye, every breath held—and Maggie felt her body go still, as if someone had cut the power.

The waitress folded the check and laid it beside the teacup, then stepped back.

Maggie pressed damp fingers to her scalp and watched the waitress's silhouette retreat. Through the blur she could make out the hostess pointing toward her with a single index finger raised.

Maggie knelt and slid her head beneath the tablecloth. She crawled on all fours, groping for her glasses, nodding as if agreeing with something unseen.

"Mommy?" Agnes said, sliding off her chair.

Before Maggie could find her bearings, Agnes dismounted to help her mother—and the deafening crunch drove the air from her warm, sticky lungs.

EVERY CELL SCREAMS

"What do you mean he hit you?" Mark said into his cell phone. The rough-sawn shiplap walls of the nursing home lobby marked the convergence of the modern and obsolete. Mark preferred to think of it as the union of prosperity and deterioration. His blood swelled and rustled. Sweat trickled from blushing glands as stomach acid crested. He regretted picking up his sister's call at all.

"Like—he hit you with his fist? Or he slapped you? Lynn?"

"What the fuck difference does it make?" she said.

"No, no. You're right. I get it. Do you want me to put Kurt on the phone? I'll talk to him."

"Talk to him? You want to talk to Kurt. On the phone?"

"What am I supposed to do, Lynn? Tell me. What do you want me to do?"

"Dammit, Mark, I don't know. You should at least want to knock his teeth in."

"I'm not sure more violence is the answer, Lynn. You could—"

"Forget it. I don't understand why I even called you. Whenever anyone is drowning, you're the first one to shore."

"Lynn, come on. That's not true. Listen—I'm heading in to visit Grandpa. Can I call you back in a half hour?"

"No, Mark. Because I have to pick up your niece from gymnastics with a bright red welt on my face and then bring her home to the guy who made it."

Mark walked to the reception desk to sign the visitor's log. From deeper in the building came faint moans and groans. The voices, he thought, were like sea creatures communicating—thick modulations of suffering trying to speak with his disquiet.

A triple-chimed grandfather clock stood next to the nurses' station. Weathered in a driftwood finish, it was dust-blanketed everywhere except the spots polished by fingerprints. The glass cabinet door—once sheltering the blackened pendulum—was cracked and spattered with mildew. Tarnished silver hands clung to the sad face. The clock clanked three times in succession.

A skinny man steeped in cheap cologne steamrolled Mark as he stared at it. The stink was an oily marriage of apple cider vinegar and crushed black pepper. The man offered no apology for the collision—or for cutting in front of Mark to ink the blank sign-in sheet.

Mark pictured himself driving the plastic pen through the man's cheek like a harpoon, the ballpoint barb visible through his teeth as he howled for help. Instead, Mark stood still and offered a polite smile as the scrawny man passed.

He could hear the murmur in his tendons. Queasy ripples in his stomach set off a tart burst of saliva at the back of his mouth. On the whole, Mark was a mixture of water and fear. The ratio shifted, but it tended toward the latter.

At door 1851, he rapped his knuckles and took a deep breath to quiet the squealing gnats in his gut. Knocking on doors made him sick—the violence of begging entrance while bracing for acceptance.

Kurt hit me, Mark. I don't know what to do.

He gripped the moist brass handle and pushed inside. The smell of decay and human excrement overwhelmed him. He was certain he could detect a note of colon cancer circulating in the room.

"Hey, Grandpa. How's it going?"

"Hi-de-ho," his grandfather said, jolted awake by the voice. "Just caught me in a snoozer here. Nice to see you, though, Mark. Come in, come in. Pull up a chair."

"I'll stand. I can't stay long."

His grandfather slumped into a checkered blue recliner. The metal arm holding the right side of the footrest tilted in its permanent state of collapse. The crooked chair made his stout frame look like a dented eggplant. An empty pillowcase was draped along the headrest—once crisp white, now burnished into mustard yellow and raw umber by years of sweat and stillness.

Nestled under the left armrest was a small circular table supported by three legs; one had been wrapped in a thick layer of white duct tape. On top sat an empty glass and a leather-bound copy of *Moby-Dick*.

"That's a fancy book, huh?" Mark said. "Where'd you get it?"

"This?" his grandfather asked. "A guy down the hall unloaded it on me. I lent him money a while back so he could get new glasses—or teeth—or something. I forget. Afterward he turned into a bag full of excuses. 'My son's coming into some coin next week. I'll have it for you tomorrow.' Blah, crap, blah. After a few weeks, he offered me the book, and I took it just to rid myself of the confrontations."

"Seems like you got screwed," Mark said.

His grandfather didn't seem to notice the dismissive tone, but Mark winced anyway. He loved his grandfather. He had fond memories. But the generational gap, and their shared sense of being bound to time, made visits feel like drudgery instead of pleasure. Today he couldn't commit to pleasantries. The tuneless humming in his brain intensified. Lynn's voice had hijacked his synapses and replaced each electrical signal with a screech.

Kurt hit me, Mark. I don't know what to do.

Mark reached for conversation to buck the silence—anything to quiet the needles and shivers performing within him.

"I've never read it. Is it any good?"

"Haven't started yet," his grandfather said, "but I promised myself I'd finish it before my interview with St. Peter."

"What the hell for?" Mark asked, his leg jackhammering. "Why *Moby-Dick*?"

"First, it's the one book I own. So there's that." He smiled faintly. "But from what I'm told, it's about this grizzled old seadog chasing a big goddamn whale that's connected to him somehow. Like they're tangled up on some larger scale. He's not just chasing it, see. It's like he is the whale. I want to see how it shakes out."

"Sounds ridiculous," Mark said, hoping to provoke a reaction. "But if it's important to St. Peter, why don't you start tonight?"

"Meh. We'll see."

Mark watched, perplexed, as his grandfather's chin plummeted toward his chest. His eyes cinched shut without effort. For a moment Mark thought he'd slipped into oblivion, but the foaming snores set him straight.

Mark was relieved he didn't have to fake conversation, but the silence made the self-reproach clearer.

Whenever anyone is drowning, you're the first one to shore.

By the time his grandfather woke, Mark's neat fingernails were gnawed bloody.

"Ugh. Sorry about that," his grandfather said after a violent, throaty snort. "All the damn medication makes me conk out like a baby forty times a day. I just go out—no warning, nothing. No control over it. But the doc tells me I have to keep taking the stuff. What am I gonna do? Tell him to shove it? Keep his poison? Who the hell am I to say anything?"

"I guess," Mark said.

"Hey—how's your sister doing? And the girls? Haven't heard from them in a while."

"They're good," Mark said. "She sent me a video of the baby walking a few weeks ago. Mandy's taking gymnastics at the middle school."

"Good, good. And Lynn?"

"I talked to her on the way here. She's... good. But I think she's having problems with Kurt."

"Problems? Like what?"

"Might be something you want to discuss with her, Grandpa."

"Oh Christ," his grandfather said. "I just told you I haven't talked to her in forever. It's not like I've moved, Mark—or got a secretary holding my calls."

"Okay. I think Kurt hit her."

His grandfather's face shifted.

"What the hell do you mean? What makes you think that?"

Mark tugged his left earlobe until cartilage popped crisply in his skull. "She told me."

"She told you." His grandfather leaned forward. "What'd she say? What about the girls?"

"She didn't say much. The girls seem fine. I don't think Kurt would do anything to the kids."

"But he did it to Lynn. What are you gonna do?"

"I don't think I'm supposed to do much of anything," Mark said. "I mean—"

"You don't think you should do anything? Who else will, Mark?"

"Listen—it's none of my business, Grandpa. They need to work it out on their own. Split up or whatever. Nothing I do will change their problems. Maybe it was a heat-of-the-moment thing. A mistake. If she was really in trouble, why would she come to me?"

"You're her brother," his grandfather said. "Her blood. And blood is thicker than water. No matter what."

"That's a cheesy cliché, Grandpa. It doesn't carry weight these days. Not in situations like this. I'm not going to butt in where I don't belong."

"What? You don't think you're part of this?"

"No. It's not my place."

His grandfather's eyes narrowed. "Listen. When I was in the Navy—"

"What does this have to do with Lynn?"

"I'm getting to it. For Christ's sake, listen." He drew a breath. "There was a guy no one would come within a shipyard of. Big corn-fed son of a bitch. One time, after trolling the Pacific for hours, we docked near one of the Mariana Islands. We came under fire. The fight ended quick on account of our numbers."

His grandfather stared past Mark, seeing it.

"We're assessing and reporting when this southern ox yells, 'What are you boys waiting for? Go get yourself a necklace.' I thought he meant jewelry—scavenging bodies. A lot of guys took souvenirs. Then, out of nowhere, he cups his hand and shoves it into the mouth of a dead enemy soldier. Fingers behind the lower teeth, thumb locked under the chin. Then he tugs."

His hand trembled once, then clenched.

"He thrashes the lifeless head back and forth—massive jerking motions. We all stood there and watched. There were guys higher rank than him. Hell, I ranked higher. But no one moved. Not a peep. We were part of something we didn't want to be part of. The war. The brotherhood. It made us prisoners. Going against your squad was like jumping overboard. The ocean was always there, ready to fill your lungs."

He swallowed.

"There were awful tearing and cracking sounds. Then that bastard's jaw is dangling in the son of a bitch's hand. Sinewy. I remember the teeth most. Unless you're a dentist, you should never see the backside of a man's teeth. It's not natural. One or two guys lost their lunches. Nobody spoke. He yelled, 'What are y'all waiting for? Get ya some.'

Honest to God, I shit my trousers right then."

His grandfather laughed once, but it came out wrong.

"I mean, now I do it a little every day. But that day it was different. I was afraid—scared of him, sure—but I was scared of myself. Why didn't I say something? Do something? Every cell in my body was screaming for me to act, but I didn't."

He looked at Mark with something like pleading.

"And guess what? It stuck. I relive it every day in everything I do. When the going gets tough, I sit still. Always have. When demons opened their eyes to look at me, I told them, 'You go ahead and do what you will. I won't be a bother. Give my warmest regards to your boss.' Sometimes I even gave the monsters a smile and a handshake."

His voice frayed.

"Every cell is still angry as hell with me, Mark. Screaming nonstop all these years. The doctors say the shitting is age and cancer. But I know the truth. It's the cells. Every tiny piece of me trying to rid itself of shame."

Without warning, his grandfather keeled over again.

The wailing of Mark's innards drowned out the snoring. He saw his opportunity to escape. For as long as he could remember, his grandfather could sense his awkwardness. At goodbyes, he used to joke, *Kiss me, and I'll whack you,* then offer his palm for a weak handshake.

This time, Mark leaned over and kissed his grandfather's pale, clammy forehead.

Kiss me, and I'll whack you, he thought.

He tiptoed out without waking him.

In the hallway and through the lobby, the dissonance inside him whirled. The buzzing in his nerves was a hundred yellow jackets trapped in a sardine tin. He paused at the vestibule door with one hand on the handle and looked back toward the sign-in desk.

The clock still registered three o'clock, but the chiming had ceased.

He stared at the hands as if they might lunge.

He took an infinite breath, pushed open the door, and reached into his pocket for his cell phone. As he dialed, the clamoring in his veins turned into a high-frequency cry. He almost hung up when he heard his brother-in-law's flat voice.

"Hey, Mark. Now's not a great time. Can I—"

"Are you home?" Mark said.

"Yeah, but—"

"Stay there. I'm coming over."

He ended the call and shut his phone off altogether. For the first time he could remember, he relished dead air. No rumble of traffic. No whir of insect wings. The electrical lines overhead carried their currents in secrecy.

Mark took the clean air into his lungs and held it.

Then he started walking.

On the way home from his sister's house, he would find the nearest bookstore and buy his own copy of *Moby-Dick*.

An iron curtain draped his nerves. His jaw unclenched. He felt the tension release.

REWIND

I used to believe that beginnings were clean. That if you traced a thing back far enough—farther than blame, farther than motive—you would find a moment untouched by consequence. A first step. A word spoken before it knew how to injure. A hand reaching without calculation. I believed this the way people believe what they need to survive a particular season of themselves.

She sat across from me at the small table by the window, stirring her coffee long after it had cooled. Outside, traffic on I-95 paused and lurched forward in uneven intervals, the sound folding in on itself. We had ordered nothing to eat. That felt intentional, though neither of us said so.

"You always do this," she said. "You rewind."

"I'm just trying to understand," I said.

She looked at me the way people do when they've heard that sentence too many times.

Understanding had once been our shared language. We used it carefully at first, like a tool that required calibration. We talked about origins—of habits, of arguments, of ourselves. We believed that if we could locate the beginning of a thing, we could avoid its ending.

This worked until it didn't.

She stopped stirring her coffee and wrapped both hands around the mug as if anchoring herself.

"Do you know what you're doing right now?" she asked.

I paused. Pausing had always felt safer than answering.

"You're stepping back," she said. "Again. You're turning this into a theory so you don't have to stay in it."

I wanted to argue. I wanted to explain that reflection wasn't escape—that it was a form of care. But the words arrived already worn, their edges softened by prior use.

"I don't think that's fair," I said.

She smiled, but it wasn't unkind. It was practiced.

"Fair isn't the point," she said. "I'm telling you how it feels."

I nodded—agreement without alteration.

For a long time, I had believed that our problems came from misunderstanding—misaligned timelines, mismatched expectations. I believed they could be solved with enough patience, enough excavation. I believed that love, properly examined, revealed its own instructions.

What I hadn't accounted for was exhaustion.

Not the dramatic kind. The quiet accumulation of moments where nothing changed because nothing was decided.

She pushed her chair back slightly. The sound it made against the floor felt louder than it should have.

"I don't need you to tell me where this comes from," she said. "I need you to tell me what you're going to do with it."

The question landed cleanly.

I opened my mouth and closed it again.

Outside, a bus exhaled at the corner. Someone laughed too loudly. Life continued without waiting for our conclusion.

"I don't know," I said.

She nodded, as if confirming something she had already suspected.

"That's what scares me," she said.

We sat there a moment longer, the beginning stretching thin, unrecognizable now. When she stood, she hesitated—not dramatically, not as a test—but as if checking whether anything would stop her.

Nothing did.

After she left, I stayed at the table and watched the surface of the coffee darken as it cooled completely. I thought about beginnings again—how rarely they announce themselves, how often they're identified only in retrospect, after they've already hardened into pattern.

I paid the bill and stepped outside.

The street looked the same as it had when we arrived. Cars moved. People passed. Somewhere, something was beginning without me.

I did not follow it.

"AULD LANG SYNE"

Tears rolled down Penny Watt's cheeks—cheeks searching for permission, or so she told herself, because the other explanation was worse. She had crossed an ocean to reach her husband and now sat beside him in a meadow outside the U.S. 15th General Hospital in Liège, just under forty miles from the Eifel and the Hürtgen Forest. The air smelled of smoke and cold metal.

Penny had boarded the U.S.S. *Texas* out of New York with no military experience and less understanding. Before she left Rhode Island, she stood on a Newport pier with other wives, watching Merchant Marine hulls nose into winter water, and told herself she would not wave goodbye twice. The Army needed nurse anesthetists. It built programs quickly, trained women quickly, moved them quickly. Penny let herself be recruited because the idea of reunion gave shape to her fear. She ricocheted from unit to unit, slipped into zones barred to "non-essential" personnel, pushed forward on a hunger that felt righteous.

And now she had reached him, and felt resistance as a physical thing, separating her from the man she had come to retrieve.

Captain Watt sat on a crate with his shoulders pitched forward, hands loose at his sides. His eyes were open but unfocused, as if he were staring at something behind Penny rather than at her. When she leaned closer, he stiffened—not with recognition, but with something like recoil.

Nearby, Nurse Maddox sat with a small circle of officers who had been trying to wring a holiday mood from the night. She lingered longer than she meant to, warmed by the attention, by the flirtation that rose in her without permission. When darkness thickened, she stood and moved away, grateful to slip from the chatter unnoticed.

Williams and Armistead were razzing Burns, enjoying the way he smiled in embarrassment in front of Nurse Maddox. Maddox laughed politely and leaned in to rescue him.

"Oh, leave the poor man alone," she said, voice soft. "He's right. War is horrible. These two gentlemen are just trying to get you all riled up." She winked at Burns. He grinned helplessly.

"Burns?" Williams scoffed. "What does Burns know about war? He's artillery. Combat belongs to infantry. Don't you know that, Nurse Maddox?"

"Let's stop talking about fighting," Armistead said. "We've got two charming ladies here and it's been a million years since we've seen anything but men with stubble. The front stinks, the cold is miserable, the lice are bad; but the worst thing is the complete absence of lovely ladies. For five months with my one good eye, to see two of them—now that's worth going to war for."

"The best thing of all?" Williams said. "No, sir. A hot bath and a fresh bandage. Then a clean white bed and actual rest. There's no comparison."

Burns spoke slowly, with a slight wheeze, as though he needed to ration his breath.

"The quiet," he said. "After you've been dug into a hole in the forest with everything exploding around you—even branches falling sounding like mortar— then you're pulled out and it goes quiet. Magnificent silence, like a record on a phonograph. The first nights of it I sat up and listened. I think I laughed. It was so damned good to hear nothing."

Armistead tossed his cigarette into the dark like a small comet. He brought his hand down on his knee with a hollow thump. Nurse Maddox leaned closer to Burns, eyes bright.

"So opinions differ," she said. "What was the worst thing, then?"

Burns's mouth opened and closed. The question didn't fit his tidy narrative. He searched for a safe answer.

From the corner of the meadow came a wheeze—unintelligible at first, then shaping itself into words. All eyes shifted. The others had nearly forgotten Captain Watt and Penny in the dark.

"What was the worst thing?" Captain Watt said. His voice sounded raw, as if scraped. "The only bad thing is the going off to war. You go, and no one tries to stop you. That's the worst thing."

Nurse Maddox stood abruptly. She had seen Captain Watt brought in bound to a stretcher, sobbing so violently the orderlies couldn't carry him without restraint. Something hideous had stripped him of reason. Maddox feared the look in his eyes because it suggested a diagnosis no one wanted to name.

She touched Burns's arm, voice sharpened with sudden purpose.

"My goodness, the horn for the last truck," she said. "Quick, Penny. We have to hurry."

They all rose. Maddox looped her arm through Penny's and urged her toward the supply truck waiting beyond the meadow. Penny resisted long enough to bend and kiss her husband's cheek.

His body convulsed under the touch.

Penny pulled back, stunned, and saw that his eyes were not soft with relief. They held something like loathing—grim, deadly, inexplicable.

Behind them, Armistead muttered that it was time to rack out. Williams lingered a moment, wanting to offer the broken officer something, anything that resembled kindness.

"You've got a hell of a nice wife, Captain," Williams said. "Real fancy.

Good for you."

Captain Watt's head lifted sharply.

"Fancy," he repeated, savoring the word as if it were poison. "Oh yes. Not one tear dropped when I left on the ship, you know. Fancy and reserved. Poor Gull's wife was fancy too. Fancy she threw roses at him that fell into the ocean and sunk, and she'd been his wife two months." He chuckled, teeth clenched against a tide of tears. "'Roses!' 'He-he!' 'See you soon, sweetie!' All so damned patriotic." His gaze locked on Williams. "Do you know what happened to Gull? I was there. Do you know?"

Armistead's face tightened. He glanced toward the medic on watch. "Come on," he said quickly, "let's get you to your rack, Captain."

Captain Watt barked a laugh that sounded like triumph.

"You don't know what happened to Gull? Well, Gull and I are standing there— two weeks out from that business in the Schmidt trenches—he's about to show me a picture of his wife when a mortar struck." Watt's words accelerated, dragging the night with them. "It was so far away we didn't even turn. Then I see something black flying toward us and Gull fell holding his wife's picture with a boot sticking out of his head. A boot. General issue. Blown two hundred yards and planted in his skull. We tried to pull it out. You think his wife would've permitted such a thing? Such a thing!"

"Shut the hell up," Armistead snapped, voice cracking. He tore himself away, cursing. The men shifted uneasily, looking at one another as if checking for permission to move.

The medic approached, trying for geniality and failing.

"You have to go to your rack now, Captain," he said. "It's a new day tomorrow. Hell, it's a new year tomorrow."

Watt's eyes gleamed at the phrase new year, as if it were obscene.

"Have to go," he repeated, nodding slowly. "We all have to go. The man who doesn't go is a coward, and they have no use for cowards.

Heroes are in style now. The chic Mrs. Gull wanted a hero to match her new Saks Fifth Avenue dress." His mouth twisted. "That's why Gull had to go and die."

He turned, searching the dim shapes around him.

"You have to let yourself be trampled on while the women look on—fancy— because it's in style now," he said, voice sinking into a strangled, complaining slur. "Isn't it sad?"

Penny stood rigid beside Nurse Maddox, arm still caught, unable to step toward her husband without being pulled away, unable to leave without feeling like she was abandoning him again. She did not know which choice was the betrayal.

Watt's gaze found her and sharpened.

"Penny was in style too," he said. "She waved goodbye with her handkerchief just like the rest."

His arms writhed upward as if calling the heavens to witness.

"The worst thing?" he said, turning toward Burns as though Burns had asked again. "The disillusionment. War is terrible. No surprise. But to find out my wife was awful, that was the worst. To see her smile and throw roses. That was the surprise. She gave up on me. She sent me!"

"But your wife is here now," Williams said, desperate. "She got on her own ship, didn't she? She tends to all of us broken fools with disregard for her own safety."

For a beat, Watt's face slackened, as if the words had passed through him without landing. Then fury surged back.

"She didn't fight for me," he said. "She didn't defend me. She drove me out. She gave me the boot—like poor Gull." His breathing quickened. "Penny has invisible barbs like a swarm of yellow jackets stinging me to maximize agony."

He jerked toward the medic as if he had remembered what medics were for.

"You're the medic," he said, voice rising. "Pull her out. Like a weed. Pull. Pull her out!"

The medic's face hardened. He gave a small signal.

Four grunts moved in.

Captain Watt fought them like a man fighting the ocean. He was wild, furious, determined to stay upright. He shook off hands that felt like rusted shackles. He screamed. His fists swung. He kicked free. It wasn't until the corporal on watch rushed in that they dragged him toward the hospital doors, his cries trailing behind him like torn cloth.

In the distance, flares hissed and burned in the sky.

The supply truck waited to return to base.

One by one, nurses and soldiers climbed in, stamping snow from boots, pulling coats tight. There was nothing for Penny to do but follow. Nurse Maddox guided her toward the truck as if moving a sleepwalker.

Penny stepped up into the bed of the truck and sat among bodies that smelled of sweat and wool and fatigue. She found her hands trembling in her lap.

As the last few climbed aboard, she began counting without meaning to, the way a person counts seconds in the dark.

"Ten... nine... eight... seven..."

The truck coughed and shuddered. The meadow receded.

Penny hummed *Auld Lang Syne* under her breath, not because she felt celebratory, but because the song gave her something to hold.

"Six... five... four... three..."

Lights in the field hospital blinked out one by one as if the structures themselves were deciding, finally, to sleep.

The moon looked like a yellow-lit ball descending a flagpole, lowering itself without ceremony.

Penny's throat tightened. She kept counting.

"Two... one..."

The truck pulled farther into night.
Everything grew still.

RESOLVED

Eli arrived early and unlocked the paint counter himself. The fluorescents were already on, humming at a pitch that made conversation feel optional. He logged into the terminal, squared the brushes, stacked lids, returned tint sticks to their slots. The machine sat quiet behind the counter, lid open, waiting.

Outside, a gull worked the dumpster lid in the wet, indifferent light.

The first customer came down the aisle holding a small square of painted drywall. It had been cut unevenly, one edge chipped where the paint had peeled away.

"I'm trying to match this," the customer said, placing it on the counter like something fragile.

Eli turned it under the lights. The color shifted with the angle—undertones appearing and disappearing as if the sample couldn't decide what it had been.

"It'll be close," Eli said. "We can get it close."

"That's fine," the customer replied. Relief, immediate and grateful.

Eli scanned the sample, selected a base, adjusted the formula by hand. The machine shook, then stopped. He hesitated before sealing the lid, thumb resting on the rim.

"If it's not quite right," he said, "you can bring it back."

The customer nodded as if the option mattered more than the paint.

At the front end, the can beeped under the scanner. The receipt printed and tore free. No one looked at it.

Back at the paint desk, Eli watched the customer linger near seasonal, then drift away again without stopping. The formula remained saved.

He didn't change it.

At deli, Rosa wrapped turkey without looking up. Malik weighed cheese, slid it on the scale twice before it landed right.

Malik nodded toward paint.

"They don't look sure."

Rosa folded the paper cleanly.

"People always look like that."

"Or they don't figure it out," Malik said.

Rosa tore the ticket and moved on. The slicer started up again, loud enough to end the thought.

In the monitor room, Darren watched paint for a moment. A customer passed, then passed again. No raised voices. No return. Nothing to log.

He waited for a problem to announce itself.

It didn't.

A few days later, the manager called Eli into the office—if a utility closet can be called that. The door stayed open. The chair across from the desk was angled slightly away, as if conversation were something that passed through, not something that remained.

"We've had a couple notes," the manager said, scrolling. "Nothing major."

Eli nodded.

"Paint returns," the manager continued. "Not high. Just recurring."

Eli waited for the question. It never arrived.

"You're handling them well," the manager said. "Offering adjustments. Being flexible. Customers like options."

"Okay," Eli said.

"Keep it up."

That was the entire meeting.

Human Resources asked Eli to step into the glass-walled office near the breakroom. Marianne smiled like she was paid by the ounce.

"This isn't formal," she said. "We just want to make sure everyone feels supported. The paint department can be high-interaction."

Eli nodded.

"If anything feels unclear," she said, "you can always escalate to a supervisor."

"Sure," Eli said.

"There's no issue," she added quickly. "This is just a check-in."

Eli thanked her and left.

Back at paint, two customers waited—one with a sample, one with a photo on a phone. Eli listened, nodded, repeated what he'd been saying all week.

"We can adjust it and get it close. If it's not right, bring it back. Lighting changes it."

Both accepted their cans and left. Eli saved two new formulas.

The next week, paint felt quieter without being quiet. Same hum, same beeps, same counter shiver when the machine ran. But the work arrived cleanly now, without the drag of revision.

Eli opened the formula archive. The list was shorter. It stayed short.

A contractor asked for eggshell white. Eli selected a preset and let the ratios populate without thinking. The lid sealed. The contractor paid and left.

A woman held up a screenshot and asked if he could make it "exactly like this." Eli chose the closest match without explaining how screens lie. She thanked him before the can even went on the shaker.

Between transactions, Eli deleted entries. He didn't reread them. He clicked, confirmed, moved on. The archive stayed tidy.

Near noon, the manager passed paint and paused the way someone pauses when they want credit for noticing.

"Returns are down," he said. "Line items are steady. Whatever changed—it's working."

"Okay," Eli said.

An email popped up that afternoon:

Team—

Just a reminder to stay consistent in our messaging. Returns are part of the

process. Let's focus on solutions and keep things positive. Thanks!

Eli read it once and closed it. The message existed, then didn't.

Darren watched paint from the monitor room. Counter clear. Aisle moving. Customers in, customers out. No linger. No return. All screens were working. Nothing to record.

A new associate shadowed Eli one morning, vest stiff, expression eager.

"I'm supposed to learn paint from you," they said.

Eli nodded and pointed to the space beside him.

"Stay here."

A customer brought up a sample. Eli scanned it quickly, selected a base, adjusted once, started the machine. The customer thanked him and left without questions.

The new associate exhaled.

"How do you know when it's right?" they asked.

Eli looked at the sealed can and the clean counter.

"You don't overwork it," he said.

"But what if they don't like it?"

Eli shrugged.

"Most people don't notice the difference."

He said it as if it were policy, not belief.

The associate nodded, relieved, and wrote something down.

A customer came in without a can.

They had photos.

They laid the phone on the counter and scrolled—half-painted wall, a seam where color shifted wrong, a corner that looked bruised under window light.

"We used the same roller," the customer said quickly. "Same paint. Same day."

Eli leaned in. He saw the unevenness. He saw the line forming behind them. He saw how long it would take to explain properly.

"Application matters," he said. "Lighting. Surface underneath."

The customer hesitated.

"It's not bad. Just... noticeable."

Eli didn't repeat the word.

"If you bring the can," he said, "we can take a look."

"Oh, I don't want to redo everything," the customer said. "I guess it's fine."

They put the phone away and left.

Eli told the manager anyway. The manager listened with his head tilted, the posture of attention without obligation.

"No physical return," he said. "No product to inspect."

"They had photos."

The manager nodded.

"Photos are subjective."

Eli waited.

"We usually need the can," the manager said. "Otherwise it's hard to verify."

"That makes sense," Eli said.

"We'll log it," the manager said, tapping his tablet. "No follow-up unless it repeats."

"Okay."

The manager smiled, satisfied with the shape of the outcome. "These things happen," he added. "Most people don't notice."

Later, Eli saw the internal dashboard entry: Customer Feedback—Resolved.

No details. No attachments. The metric beside it held steady.

He clicked once. Nothing expanded.

A laminated card appeared on the inside edge of the counter:
Recommended Presets Standard matches encouraged
Limited adjustments available for complex requests,
schedule a consultation.

A QR code sat at the bottom like a punchline.

Customers paused, read, and kept walking. Some took paint off the shelf and never approached the counter at all.

Eli watched one of them hesitate with a sample in hand, glance at the code, then put the sample back and select a white.

The customer left as if the aisle had never existed.

"I'm moving up front," Rosa told Malik one morning.

"Good," Malik said too quickly. "Quieter."

Rosa nodded, eyes on the slicer.

"More predictable."

There was no announcement. No last shift. By week's end, someone else stood where Rosa had been.

Malik trained the new hire without explaining why anything was done the way it was.

"You keep the stack neat," he said. "People like to see it that way."

"And if they hesitate?" the new hire asked.

Malik looked out toward paint, then away.

"They usually don't," he said. "Just keep moving."

He didn't mention Rosa again.

The manager called Eli in one more time.

"We want to leverage you," he said. "Cross-training. Floating. Supporting other departments."

"That's fine," Eli replied.

He signed the schedule change without reading it closely.

When he passed paint later, the counter was empty. The sign remained. The QR code remained. The preset sheet had replaced the laminated card—smaller font, tighter language.

A customer brought in a sample that made the new associate pause.

"This one's tricky," they said.

"But the preset is close," they added, already selecting it.

The machine started. The counter vibrated. The decision sealed itself.

Eli stood there a moment, then moved on.

In the monitor room, Darren watched a full shift pass without interruption. The screens cycled smoothly. Paint appeared for a few seconds, then gave way to deli, dairy, seasonal, front end. Everything flowed.

Darren checked the log twice out of habit, then stopped checking the time between entries. The sheet stayed blank long enough that blank began to feel like success.

At the front end, the cashier called:

"Next."

The word landed cleanly.

A customer stepped forward with a return. The cashier followed prompts without looking at the item.

"That'll go back to your card."

The receipt printed. The line advanced.

Inside the store, the cameras continued to cycle.

The counters stayed clean.

The presets held.

Nothing waited to be seen.

OPEN MIC

The chalkboard by the door said **BE NICE** in bubble letters that had started to sag at the corners, like the room itself didn't quite believe it anymore.

Steven paused under it anyway, out of habit, the way people pause beneath a sign even when they don't intend to obey. The bar was narrow and long, wood-darkened by years of elbows and spilled liquor. A strand of white Christmas lights blinked along the ceiling, out of season, a kind of permanent apology for the lighting. The air smelled like citrus cleaner and old beer, and underneath that, the sweet heat of bodies packed too close. Through the front window, headlights crawled past on Route 6, smeared by winter salt.

The host—a man with a tidy beard and the calm, managerial smile of someone who had learned to steer chaos with a microphone—looked up from his clipboard.

"You on the list?" he asked, already scanning Steven's face for the right category of person.

Steven nodded toward the back. "Just here to watch."

"Good man," the host said, and then, as though remembering the sign: "Keep it kind tonight."

Steven drifted toward the small stage—a low platform with a mic stand and a stool that looked like it had survived three different divorces. A few people were already seated with their drinks angled defensively toward their chests. Others stood in the shadows near the bathrooms, where the door frames were pocked from years of shoulder-checking.

Veronica was at a corner table with her notebook open, pen cap between her teeth. She looked up when Steven approached and smiled with the mild strain of someone already half onstage in their mind.

"Hey," Steven said.

"Hey," she replied. The smile held, then softened. "You made it."

"Of course." Steven slid into the chair beside her. "You're up tonight?"

Veronica tapped the paper twice, as though knocking on the wood of the table. "If I don't leave the building first."

Steven's laugh came out too loud, and Veronica's eyes flicked toward the stage, then back. She wasn't joking. Not fully.

The host's voice rose over the room. "Alright, alright—welcome, people. This is open mic. This is a listening room. You're going to clap like you mean it, you're going to tip your bartender, and you're going to treat everybody on this stage like a human being. We got enough other places in the world for the opposite."

A smattering of applause, more polite than sincere, moved through the crowd like a weak wave. The host smiled and kept going anyway, because that's what hosts did: they announced the rules as though rules could keep a room from becoming itself.

Steven leaned toward Veronica. "You nervous?"

Veronica's eyes stayed on her notebook. "I'm—" She stopped, searching for the correct word, the honest one. "I'm trying to be brave in public."

"That's a dumb requirement," Steven said.

"Yeah," Veronica murmured. "But apparently it's the hobby."

Onstage, a man with an acoustic guitar fumbled through a song about being misunderstood. The room listened in fragments—half attention, half evaluation. Laughter arrived in the wrong places. The bartender moved with practiced speed, the sort of speed that meant nothing here ever fully stopped.

Steven watched the crowd the way you watched weather. There were the eager ones, faces tilted toward the stage like hungry dogs. There were the skeptical ones, arms crossed, chin lifted, waiting to be convinced. And there were the people who had come to be seen, not to see: bodies turned sideways to the performance so they could keep an eye on who was watching them watch.

When the guitar guy finished, the applause was generous in the way pity can be generous.

The host bounced back onstage. "Give it up, give it up—alright! Next we have Cal."

Steven felt Veronica's shoulder tighten. She didn't look at him. She didn't have to.

Cal walked up with the confidence of a man entering a room he believed he owned. He had the kind of smile that asked for trust and made it your fault if you gave it. He adjusted the mic stand dramatically, as if height mattered more than content.

"Hey," Cal said, and the room responded with a small cheer, a familiarity that made Steven's stomach go faintly sour. Cal was a regular. A known quantity. The sort of man you could describe as "harmless" right up until he wasn't.

"I was thinking," Cal began, "about how everyone's always talking about trauma."

A few laughs—already. Steven watched them land. People laughed not because the line was funny but because Cal had said the right word with the right tone, and the room liked recognizing itself as current.

"And I don't want to be insensitive," Cal continued, holding both hands up like he was surrendering. "But if everyone's got trauma, isn't that just… life?"

More laughter. A woman near the front clapped once, delighted, like

Cal had cleaned up a messy cultural conversation with a sponge.

Veronica's pen stopped moving. Her eyes fixed on Cal like she was waiting for a car to hit her—bracing, helpless, certain.

Cal launched into a story about an ex who "weaponized therapy language" and "gas-lit him" with boundaries. He imitated her voice, high and nasal. The room laughed. Steven felt his own face warming, anger arriving with the quiet shame of being late.

"Like," Cal said, "she's talking about 'safe spaces'—and I'm like, babe, the world is not a safe space. The world is a bar bathroom."

The crowd roared at that. Steven heard the laughter and thought of the chalkboard: **BE NICE**.

Cal leaned into it. "And you know what she wrote once? She wrote: 'I want a love that doesn't make me smaller.'"

Steven's throat tightened. Veronica had written that line. Steven had heard her read it, voice steady and furious, weeks ago in their kitchen, her hands shaking around a mug.

Cal didn't pause. He delivered it as a punchline.

"And I'm like—fine. Go date a... what, a cloud? Go date the ocean. Go date a chair."

The room laughed harder, grateful for the permission. Steven's eyes snapped to Veronica. Her face had gone still in a way that wasn't calm. Stillness as self-defense.

Cal continued, and each new "joke" was a detail Steven recognized: the way Veronica kept her keys between her fingers when she walked at night; the scar on her inner wrist she covered with bracelets; the habit of saying "I'm fine" with a smile sharp enough to cut glass.

None of the details were blatant enough to be actionable. That was the trick.

He wasn't saying her name. He was letting the people who mattered know, and letting everyone else enjoy the cruelty without the discomfort of certainty.

Steven felt the urge to stand, to interrupt, to do something messy and obvious.

He didn't. He stayed seated, the way people stay seated when the room is already applauding.

Cal ended to a standing ovation from three drunk guys near the bar. The host hugged him with exaggerated warmth, microphone still live.

"Give it up for Cal!" the host shouted. "That's how you do it!"

Steven watched Veronica close her notebook with careful precision, as if slamming it would cause an explosion. She opened it again. Her hands were steady. She looked like someone trying to keep her body from betraying her in public.

The host glanced at his list. "Alright—Veronica?"

Veronica stood before Steven could speak. Her chair scraped the floor louder than it should have. She walked to the stage with her shoulders straight, posture like a dare.

Steven's stomach clenched. He knew the room would compare them. He knew the room would decide, silently, whether Veronica was "a good sport." He knew Cal was watching from the edge of the platform, smiling like he'd bought a ticket to the show he'd just forced her to perform.

Veronica adjusted the mic once and looked out at the crowd. She didn't smile.

"Hi," she said.

A few people murmured hello back, as if politeness could cover what had just happened.

Veronica's eyes found Steven for a brief second—not a plea, not a check-in. Something more like: witness.

She unfolded a page.

"My poem is called 'Small.'"

The room quieted in the uneven way rooms quiet: not from reverence, but from curiosity. Silence as a reset button.

Veronica read, voice low and clear:

"I want a love that doesn't make me smaller—not a hand on the back of my

neck guiding me into a photograph

I didn't agree to be in."

A few people shifted. Someone laughed once—an embarrassed cough of sound—and then stopped when no one joined.

Veronica continued:

"Not a joke made with my name removed.

Not a story where I'm the twist.

Not applause that lands on me like a verdict."

Steven felt his breath catch. The room wasn't laughing. Not now. They were listening, and listening looked like discomfort when the content demanded a cost.

From the corner of his eye, Steven saw Cal's smile tighten.

Veronica didn't look at him. She read as if Cal didn't exist, which was a kind of violence, too.

"When you say 'it's not that deep,'

what you mean is:

don't make me responsible

for what I already know I did."

A woman near the front lowered her drink. The bartender paused mid-pour. The room was still—not peaceful, not kind, but held.

Veronica finished without flourish.

"Thank you," she said, voice even, and stepped back from the mic.

There was a beat. One of those beats where a room decides what version of itself it will be.

Applause came, but it was fractured. Some people clapped hard, almost angrily, as if trying to prove they weren't complicit. Others offered the slow, polite claps reserved for funerals and school recitals. A few didn't clap at all, eyes down, as if silence could absolve them.

The host hurried onstage and laughed too loudly. "Alright! Woo! That was—okay, that was beautiful. See? We got all kinds of talent in here."

He leaned toward Veronica and murmured something Steven couldn't hear, but his smile stayed fixed. He guided her offstage like a customer being escorted away from a problem.

Veronica returned to the table and sat. Her hands shook now that she was seated, small tremors she couldn't discipline away.

Steven leaned in. "That was—"

"Don't," Veronica said quietly.

He stopped.

Across the room, Cal approached a cluster of regulars, already shaping his next story with his hands. He glanced toward Veronica and Steven once, quick as a surveillance check, then turned away, satisfied.

The host called another performer. The show continued. That was the room's greatest skill: continuation.

Steven sat with Veronica through two more acts. He watched her pretend to listen, her eyes fixed somewhere beyond the stage. When someone told a joke about "crazy exes," Veronica's fingers tightened around her glass until her knuckles went pale.

During a break, Steven stood. "I'm going to talk to him."

Veronica's eyes snapped to his. "Don't."

"I can't just—"

"You can," she said. The word landed like a slap. "That's what everyone does. That's the whole thing."

Steven felt heat rise in his chest. Shame and anger braided together.

"I'm not everyone," he said, too defensively.

Veronica's voice dropped. "If you make it a scene, he wins twice. Once for the joke, once for the drama. And I'm the—" She swallowed. "I'm the story again."

Steven sat back down, jaw tight.

Veronica looked at him with something like exhaustion. "If you want to do something," she said, "don't do it in front of an audience."

Steven waited until the next performer started, until the room's attention shifted, then stood and moved through the tables. The bathroom hallway was crowded with smoke and laughter. The chalkboard sign was visible from here too, glowing with its dumb optimism.

Cal was at the bar with his phone out, already replaying something, laughing with the bartender. The bartender laughed back because laughing was part of the job.

Steven stopped beside him. "Hey."

Cal glanced up. "Hey, man. Great crowd tonight, right?"

Steven kept his voice low. "You used Veronica's lines."

Cal's smile didn't leave. It adjusted, smaller, more patient. "What?"

"You quoted her," Steven said. "You used her stuff."

Cal's brows lifted in exaggerated innocence. "Dude, I didn't say her name."

"That's not the point." Steven felt his pulse thudding in his neck. "You knew exactly what you were doing."

Cal leaned back against the bar, relaxed. He looked past Steven toward the stage, as if Steven were blocking his view of the real show.

"Listen," Cal said, voice mild, "I talk about my life. She talks about her life. Life overlaps. Everybody's stealing from everybody."

Steven stared at him. "That's convenient."

Cal's eyes sharpened for a second—just long enough for Steven to see the edge underneath the "nice guy" varnish.

"You her boyfriend?" Cal asked.

Steven didn't answer.

Cal smiled again. "Then it's not really your fight."

Steven's hand tightened into a fist at his side. He forced it open. He didn't want to be the story, either. He wanted the room to behave differently without making noise. He wanted to fix harm with the right tone.

"You're a coward," Steven said quietly.

Cal laughed, soft. "Okay."

Steven swallowed. "You humiliated her."

Cal's mouth twisted like he was almost bored. "Nobody forced her to go onstage. If she didn't like it, she could've stayed home."

Steven felt something in him go cold—an internal click, like a lock engaging.

Before he could speak again, the host appeared beside them, smile bright.

"Everything good here?" the host asked, voice cheerful, eyes scanning Steven the way bouncers scan drunk men for potential.

Steven looked at the host. "No."

The host kept smiling. "Okay. But we're doing a show, so let's—"

"You put him on," Steven said. "You heard him."

The host's smile tightened. "Hey. We don't police comedy. This is a space for voices."

"Whose?" Steven asked.

The bartender set down a drink hard enough to rattle ice. The sound was small but sharp.

Cal leaned forward, almost friendly. "Man, you're making it weird."

The host's voice lowered. "If you've got a complaint, you can email the venue."

Steven stared at him. "That's your solution."

The host's eyes flicked, annoyed now. "We have to keep things moving."

Steven thought of continuation. The room's greatest skill.

He stepped back. "Right," he said, and walked away before he did something loud.

When he returned to Veronica's table, she didn't ask what happened.

She could read it on his face: the system had run; the outcome had been predetermined.

"I'm sorry," Steven said.

Veronica's laugh was thin. "For what? For finding out bars don't have ethics?"

"For not stopping it," Steven said.

Veronica's eyes softened, just slightly. "You can't stop a room," she said. "You can only decide what you'll tolerate from it."

Steven nodded, throat tight.

They left before the show ended. Outside, the night air was cold and damp, the street glistening under the lamplights. The bar's laughter leaked out every time the door opened, then snapped shut like a mouth.

They walked in silence for two blocks.

Finally, Veronica said, "He'll tell that story again."

Steven nodded. "Yeah."

"And the room will laugh again," she said.

"Yeah."

Veronica stopped under a streetlight and looked at Steven. Her face held no tears. Her voice was steady.

"Do you know what the worst part is?" she asked.

Steven waited.

"It's not that he did it," Veronica said. "It's that everyone else wants to be the kind of person who laughs at it without being guilty."

Steven felt the sentence settle in his chest like a stone.

When he got home, he couldn't sleep. He lay in the dark and listened to the familiar sounds of the house—plumbing, refrigerator, the thin whisper of traffic far away.

Around one in the morning, his phone buzzed.

A text from someone he barely knew: a guy Veronica had once introduced as "a regular."

It was a link.

Steven clicked it and watched a short video, shaky and overexposed. Cal onstage, laughing. Cal saying, "I want a love that doesn't make me smaller—" and the room exploding with laughter as if they'd been starving for it.

In the corner of the frame, barely visible, Veronica's face—still, lit by the stage light, eyes fixed ahead.

Steven watched the clip twice, then set the phone down face-up on the bed like evidence he couldn't submit anywhere.

In the morning, Veronica would go to work. Cal would tell the story again. The host would smile and call it community.

The chalkboard would still say **BE NICE**.

And the room would keep moving.

Steven lay there and listened to his own breathing, heavy in the quiet.

He understood, finally, that applause wasn't praise.

It was a verdict.

THE BALLROOM

I woke up on the carpet of an empty ballroom at Foxwoods in Connecticut with the jingle still rattling around in my head and the taste of copper in my mouth.

Let's live, for the wonder, of it all…

The lights were half on, dimmed to a tired glow, humming like insects trapped in glass. The room was too large for one body. Rows of tables sat folded against the walls like obedient furniture waiting to be told what shape to take. The air smelled faintly of bleach and something sweeter beneath it—spilled liquor ground into fabric.

People call it excessive. I've always preferred "problem drinking." It leaves a door open. Alcoholism sounds like a verdict handed down in a room I'm not allowed to speak in.

I lay there a moment longer than necessary, testing my limbs, listening for footsteps. The ballroom absorbed sound the way a church does. Every shift of my weight felt amplified, then swallowed.

I imagined the room alive again. Music pulsing. Couples rotating under soft lights. Dresses brushing ankles. Shoes polished just enough to suggest intention. My shadow stretched long across the carpet, thin and distorted, the only thing moving with purpose.

The nausea came in waves, each one promising release and delivering none. I swallowed hard and rolled onto my side. The carpet was damp in places, gritty with dirt tracked in from outside. I pressed my palm into it and thought, absurdly, of how many shoes had crossed this floor without stopping.

The wonder of it.

Hours earlier, the bar across the casino floor had closed and taken everyone with it. I'd spoken to someone there—nothing memorable, nothing that would linger. By now, I was already gone from their night. The room had moved on. I crossed the casino and ended up in the ballroom—empty, hushed, too large for one person.

I stared up at the columns lining the walls, ornate and chipped, their carved leaves frozen mid-fall. Yellow, red, gold—colors meant to suggest abundance. Outside, winter would beat them down again. They would never finish their descent.

I wanted to gather them. I wanted to put them somewhere safe.

Drinking feels contractual. It's how people agree to be near one another without explanation. Quitting feels like breaking terms. Not dramatic ones—small ones. Who you meet after work. Where you stand at parties. How long you stay.

The thought of sobriety makes my skin tighten. It isn't the absence of drink that scares me—it's the presence of myself. Unbuffered. Awkward. Left with whatever I've been avoiding. I imagine hours stretching out with nothing to soften them. I imagine myself speaking and hearing it all land wrong.

Maybe that's what living looks like.

The memory snaps back without warning.

I'm upright now, stumbling, my phone slipping from my hand as my body lurches forward. Panic grabs me by the throat. I gag and retch until a thin line of bile hits the carpet, bright and humiliating. My hands claw at the floor, fibers catching under my nails.

I scan the room for cameras. For proof. For someone who might be watching. Beneath the panic is something older.

The smell of the carpet—stale and sour—matches the rug beneath my childhood bed where I once hid. It's the same smell as the hallway carpet in the rectory where I went looking for help and found something else waiting. Those memories rise without sound, filling my chest until breathing feels optional.

Not voices. Not madness. Just a hum—roles, masks, lies—fear vibrating beneath everything.

I push myself toward the exit. Public space hits hard and fast. People pass by, already moving somewhere else, carrying their own weight. I lower my head and move through them, smaller than I remember being.

It isn't just how I look that makes them stare. Melancholy is common. This is something else—an atmosphere I drag behind me. Despair that brushes up against strangers and lingers.

I never belonged in that ballroom.

Even now, as I walk away, something tugs at me. Not redemption. Not resolve. Just the quiet pull of a room large enough to disappear in, ready to be filled again.

THE WEIGHT OF SOUND

When Emma woke, she searched the dark for the man beside her.

Since the Shift, the darkness felt evacuated—an ocean after the tide has pulled out, leaving only wet shine and the smell of something gone. She slid her palms over the blankets until she found Noah's steady heartbeat. Only then did she let herself sit up.

Morning came in bruised pink through the blinds. She waited—an old superstition now—for her shadow to stretch across the floorboards. Sometimes she could convince herself it did.

Most nights, she dreamed of being buried.

Not the dramatic kind—no coffin, no screaming—just soil patiently heaped over her, roots looping her ankles and climbing her ribs with the intimacy of vines. In the dream she recognized them: the same roots from her garden at home, the small patch where her son had once pressed seeds into dirt with sticky hands and declared, with absolute conviction, that they'd grow.

She always woke with her mouth open, lungs trying to drink air that felt too quiet to be real.

On her way to the window she paused in the hallway. A floorboard exhaled a slow creak.

"Just settling," she whispered—automatic, the way you speak to yourself when you need the house to remain a house.

But the sound had rhythm, like weight shifting.

Noah stirred.

"You alright?" he murmured, voice rough.

Emma nodded, though she hadn't answered. She slipped on her boots and left before he could sit up fully.

She took her usual loop of Main Street: down past the harbor, then up toward the scenic overlook where the highway unspooled for miles with no traffic to prove it was still a highway. At the pier, she stopped and listened.

For a second she thought she heard it again—that thin humming, a child's tune, simple as thread. It pressed at the base of her skull, then thinned and vanished.

Emma held her breath to catch it.

The wind carried only brine.

She walked home anyway, as though returning could undo what she'd heard.

Inside, she built a fire, boiled potatoes, poured water into her husband's old French press. When the metal filter hissed, Noah jolted awake like a man slapped.

"You hear that?" he whispered.

"It's just coffee."

He settled back carefully, as though his body might disturb something unseen. Emma peeled potatoes and watched him breathe, then glanced out to the street, hoping for movement—someone, anyone, a mistake in the world's emptiness.

Nothing.

The quiet in the house felt dense, not peaceful—pressure, like a hand pressed over the mouth of the day.

"Morning," he muttered when he finally sat up.

"I'm still here," she said.

After breakfast, they set out by bicycle. The streets were empty, the silence loud in the way it gets right before a storm breaks.

"You doing alright?" Noah asked.

Emma almost laughed. Instead she said, "Living the dream," because sarcasm was easier than language with edges.

They'd decided to push farther today. The library marked half a day's travel. This time they'd cross the stream behind it and keep going until either they found someone alive or their hope finally ran out of fuel. They strapped camping gear to their carts and pedaled.

Noah cleared his throat. In the stillness, the sound felt violent.

"You ever feel like they're still… around?" he asked.

Emma nearly snapped—No one is around—but swallowed it. The truth, when she held it in her mouth, tasted metallic.

Near dusk they found an old farmer's market. Windows intact. Cars frozen in place. A flag bristled as though breath had been caught in the fabric and left there.

Emma scavenged expired seed packets from a dusty shelf. She could coax life from worse. She could make something grow if she had to. It was a kind of religion.

Down a narrow aisle, Noah stopped beneath a sagging beam. His eyes darted left-right-left, as if tracking movement he couldn't see.

"You okay?" Emma asked.

He blinked, startled by her voice. "I tried to open the door," he whispered, as though confessing. "Never mind."

"What door?"

"There were too many," he said, softer. "I was only one person."

"What do you hear?" she pressed.

"Nothing," he said too fast.

Outside, behind the building, Emma found a baby seat crusted with mold. The straps were stiff. She buckled them with trembling hands anyway, as if the act could bring the child back into it—as if the posture of care mattered even when there was no one left to receive it.

A faint hum threaded the air—the same child's melody. It pressed behind her ears like fingers.

"Noah—"

"Stop," he said.

Stop what? She hadn't moved.

They left the market and cut through a stand of trees. On the far side, the world looked untouched—no wires, no litter, no signs that people had ever tried to build permanence here.

That was what made it wrong.

"Left?" Emma asked when the path forked.

"Sure."

They set camp by large rocks, tucked between pine shadows and open sky. Noah wrapped his arms around her. She felt only the preservation of heat, not comfort. His breath was warmer than hers—too warm.

She pulled away.

"Are you cold?" he asked.

"No. You?" It was frostbitten cold for her—bone-deep, the kind that made the body feel like a poorly insulated house. But Noah's skin felt summer-warm.

He shook his head. "I can't feel it."

Inside the tent, silence pressed its ear to the fabric. No crickets. No wind. Even the forest seemed to be holding itself still.

They ate tinned food packaged by hands now dust. Noah chewed softly, but even that tiny sound felt heavy, as if each bite had weight. Books were opened but not read. Eventually Noah slept.

Emma did not.

She nudged him.

"What?" he mumbled, half awake. "What's wrong?"

"Why do you think this happened?" Her voice cracked on the last word, betraying the childishness of the question—as if the world could have a reason that fit inside a sentence.

Noah blinked. "I don't know. I'm tired, Em."

"Are we just together forever now?"

"I suppose."

"What do you mean?"

He rolled onto his back, eyes open to the dark. "We're in this together," he murmured, voice hollow, like someone reciting an oath he no longer believed in.

Emma stared at the blackness above them.

"Do you think we'll find anyone else?"

"Maybe." A pause. "Do you miss them?"

"Not the violent ones."

"No… your boy. Your husband."

Emma's throat tightened. She swallowed once, hard, as if she could push the memory back down.

"He said he'd take him farther into the water," she whispered. The confession escaped her like a cough. "I said no. I always said no."

In the dark she saw it again: summer glare on the cove, the bright cruelty of sunlight on water, her husband's easy confidence, her son's laughter pitched high with trust. She had watched them wade. She had watched, and in watching had somehow believed that attention was a form of control.

Silence widened until it felt physical—thick as wool.

Somewhere beyond the treeline: tap… tap-tap… tap.

Emma sat up, heart thudding.

"You hear that?" she whispered.

Noah's eyes were open already, staring past her. "They're still knocking," he said.

She listened. Nothing. No tapping. Only her own breath, and even that felt like an intrusion.

The absence of sound weighed more than the tap ever could.

Dawn arrived pale and skeletal. Cold clung. Emma wandered from camp until the tent was a small shape behind her, until she felt briefly—

ridiculously—like she might be the last person alive in a world that didn't want witnesses.

As the sun crested, she lifted her palms skyward.

"Why am I still here?" she whispered. "I shouldn't have to be without them."

Her breath vanished in the air.

By afternoon they found a strip plaza: barren storefronts, a lone corpse collapsed beside a window like discarded clothing.

"You think that's the owner?" Emma asked.

Noah's jaw tightened. "Who cares?"

"Someone dreamed this place," Emma said. "Built it from nothing."

"Everything's gone, Em."

"If she's the owner," Emma said, "she'll spend eternity staring into her own empty windows."

"Jesus," Noah snapped. "Knock it off."

Emma stared at the blank glass. She thought of the way people built and built as if building were a spell against death.

"I'd rather live inside a dream than rot beside it," she said.

A glass door rattled behind them.

Windless.

Noah spun, breath sharp. Emma heard only the rustle of her sleeve; the quiet after made her skin prickle.

"They moved," he whispered.

"Who?"

He didn't answer.

They walked on. Emma's mind drifted—summer days at the cove; music humming through warm air; her boy's laughter; her husband singing off-key on purpose to make the child squeal. She never let them wade too far. Fear had always been her private governor. Sometimes in the silence, a hum returned—familiar, infectious—and when she turned, there was only Noah.

Eventually rows of identical houses emerged like teeth.

"Who lived this close together?" Noah muttered.

"Let's look around."

Emma hunted blankets and scarves; warmth was her currency. She moved through houses with the practiced hunger of someone learning what she could live without. Then—without warning—the hush.

Not silence: a halt.

As if something had been humming just out of reach and abruptly stopped.

The pressure behind her ears released all at once. At the same moment, Noah lifted his hands to his own ears.

"Please," he said, to no one.

Emma felt her pulse crawl.

She pushed open a swollen door. Inside: a child's bedroom. Toy chest. Woodland animals painted on the wall. Dust-stuffed foxes stared from shelves with their stitched eyes.

And then the lullaby swelled between the boards.

It wasn't loud, but it filled the room the way water fills a glass. It trapped breath in Emma's ribs, heavy as guilt.

Behind her, Noah's shadow stretched across the mural—longer than his body, warped by an unseen mass.

"You okay?" he asked.

Emma reached out and touched the painted fox. Warmth bloomed beneath her fingers, immediate and impossible, like a living thing responding. The lullaby cut off as if someone had placed a hand over its mouth. Silence smothered the room, thick and absolute.

Outside, hundreds of houses waited—dreams abandoned mid-breath.

"You ever think I'm not supposed to leave?" Emma whispered. "Part of me stayed."

Noah stepped close.

"You left because you were alive," he said.

She almost said her husband's name, but stopped, the way you stop yourself from touching a bruise.

"And you?" she asked instead.

Noah looked away.

That night Emma counted breaths. Inhale—heavy. Exhale—too light. Between breaths, she understood something she'd been refusing: she was alone. Had always been. Her son. Her husband. The melodies. The footsteps. All of it—the world's insistence that something was still near.

Noah startled.

She sat up.

"Where were you during the Shift?" she asked.

Noah didn't answer at first. His outline in the dark seemed thinner than it should have been, like a picture held at the wrong angle.

"You know," he said.

"Tell me."

Noah swallowed. "I was already gone," he said softly. "You just took me with you."

Emma stared at him, waiting for her mind to reject the sentence.

"Am I dead?" she whispered.

"No," he said. "You're haunted."

Morning thinned his shape. Edges frayed. Even the air around him felt thicker, as if sound clung to his fading outline—the way dust clings to a hand that doesn't belong anywhere anymore.

"You can stay," he whispered. "Live inside echoes… or you can walk home."

Emma thought of the baby seat. The roots in her dreams. The way grief buried you slowly, politely, one shovel of day at a time.

She stood.

"I'll walk."

Noah's smile was tired, almost relieved.

"Good."

He dissolved into silence, and it felt like a weight lifting from the world—not joy, not peace, but the end of a pressure you'd forgotten you were resisting.

Emma took the long road back—past the strip plaza, the market, the graveyard of lives unlived. Silence followed her. It behaved like an unstaffed switchboard: no signals, no replies—just the line staying open.

At her family home, the morning clouds blushed pink again, as if the sky refused to learn.

Emma opened the shutters wide and let the light in.

This time, her shadow stretched across the floor.

For the first time since the Shift, Emma cast a shadow.

INTERLUDE

Somewhere along the way I stopped remembering in chapters. I started remembering in fragments: a line, a look, the way a room sounded after someone left it. The same moment would come back, not identical—just remastered. That's what replay is: not repetition, but insistence. A story can end and still keep playing. At a certain point, the only honest way to hold it is to press it into a record and let it spin.

* * *

THE SOUNDTRACK OF THE IN-BETWEEN

THE SOUNDTRACK OF THE IN-BETWEEN

A two-sided record in twelve tracks
by Jude Carver
(Performed by Miles Skye)

Track-list

SIDE A — The Waiting Room
   Track 01 — *Tiny House Theory*
   Track 02 — *Halo*
   Track 03 — *Number Three*
   Track 04 — *Why Am I Not the One*
   Track 05 — *Inkwell*
   Track 06 — *Next to Nowhere*

SIDE B — Terms & Light
   Track 07 — *VIP Black Gucci*
   Track 08 — *Turn Around*
   Track 09 — *Streetlight Secrets*
   Track 10 — *New Jersey & Florida*
   Track 11 — *Frozen Desire*
   Track 12 — *Failing Heart*

Liner Notes

If you're holding this, it means you stopped long enough to listen. So, thanks.

I wrote most of this album in places that don't make it into stories: behind venues, in motel beds that smell like bleach, in the passenger seat while my friend drove and pretended not to watch me fall apart. Some nights the room felt holy. Most nights it didn't.

People like to tell you you're "close." They say it like it's a compliment, like "close" is a place you can live. But close is a hallway. Close is a hand on the doorknob that never turns all the way.

These tracks aren't about winning. They're about what happens when you keep chasing anyway—and how you start to confuse movement with meaning. If you hear yourself in it, I'm sorry. If you hear someone you love in it, call them.

—Miles

SIDE A — THE WAITING ROOM

Track 01 — Tiny House Theory

I have been searching for something ugly
because the pretty things make me feel bad.
I have been searching for the shy ones, the silent ones.
They do not speak unless they have something deep to say.
I will live small with a few good books
and this old six-string.
I will turn my back on the status quo.

The first sound of morning is always the same: a small appliance in a cheap room doing its best impression of purpose.

The heater rattles like it's got a secret. The ice machine down the hall coughs and resets. Somewhere, a faucet runs too long—the private, stubborn music of a stranger rinsing off last night. You learn to name these things when you live out of bags. Not because it's romantic, but because naming is what you do when you need the world to feel slightly less unmoored.

I wake up before the alarm, because touring trains your body to expect harm in the form of opportunity. The set is done. The money is counted. The night is over. And still, the next day stands in the doorway like a promoter with a clipboard: Up. Move. Prove it again.

The room smells like stale detergent and the kind of soap that tries too hard. The curtains are a shade of brown that only exists in places nobody intends to remember. On the nightstand, my phone lies face-down, as if it's embarrassed to deliver the same non-news every morning: no miracles, no messages, no sudden change in my place in the universe.

I turn it over anyway. I'm not above superstition. I've begged emptiness for less.

No new notifications. No label rep. No manager. No divine voicemail.

Just the time, glaring: 6:12 a.m.

I sit up slowly because my head is a workshop where last night's noise is still being assembled into regret. We played a sticky little room with a bar that sells wings and scratch tickets. Forty-something people came through, and for ninety minutes I managed to convince them—convince myself—that I was doing something closer to living than drifting.

Afterward, someone hugged me with both arms and said, "Man, you should be bigger than this."

It's the working songwriter's favorite compliment, because it's praise and tragedy in the same breath. It's also the easiest kind of love to accept. It doesn't ask anything of you except to keep being a story.

I swing my legs off the bed. My jeans are in a heap near the chair, my shirt draped over the lamp like a surrender flag. On the chair is my notebook, open and face-up, like a witness. I don't remember taking it out, which means I did. I only write when the day won't let me sleep.

The page is a mess of ink: arrows, scratched-out lines that look like they were punched through the paper. There are fragments. A chorus I'll never finish. A single phrase circled three times.

And, at the bottom, written like a joke I told myself while half-asleep: tiny house

I stare at those two words as if they're coordinates. Not because I actually believe in the tiny house as a solution—but because it's the cleanest version of the life I want.

Small. Quiet. Mine.

No velvet ropes. No "exposure." No smile held too long for a photo. No sugar-high praise from strangers that evaporates the minute you need an actual friend.

Just a door that locks. A few shelves of good books. A table where I can set down my guitar and not worry someone's going to trip over the case and break the only thing I own that feels loyal.

I can picture it too easily, which is how I know it's a real hunger. A narrow little place tucked somewhere near water or woods—someplace where the nights are dark enough to deserve the stars. I'm not picky about geography; touring killed that part of me. But my body still speaks Rhode Island in its sleep: salt air that clings to your clothes, the way Route 1 looks in winter, the way Providence glows when you come over the hill on I-95 and the city pretends it's larger than it is.

A laugh escapes me. It comes out wrong—more cough than humor.

I get up and cross the room. The mirror over the sink is speckled with old water stains, as if it's tired of reflecting people who don't recognize themselves in the morning. I splash cold water on my face. My eyes look older than the rest of me, which is not a poetic thing—just the reality of living on caffeine and hope and whatever you can eat at midnight without hating yourself.

When I'm done, I stand there with the towel in my hands, listening to the building. It creaks. It settles. It sighs like a tired animal.

I check my phone again. Still nothing.

I check it a third time because I'm apparently committed to humiliation as a morning ritual.

Still nothing.

On the nightstand beside the phone is the flyer from last night's show. It's folded, smudged. Someone spilled something on it. My name is

printed in bold, the font trying to do the heavy lifting of significance:
MILES SKYE
(As if a last name like that is a promise instead of a joke.)

I pick it up. On the back, in the same frantic hand, I've written something I don't remember writing:

I'm trying to run away from the status quo.

I read it twice, then a third time. It doesn't sound like a lyric. It sounds like a confession—like something a man says when he's quietly afraid he's already been caught.

Status quo. Such a harmless phrase. Like a couch you don't love but keep sitting on because it's familiar. Like a job that doesn't kill you—only slowly convinces you not to want anything.

I used to believe the status quo was what happened to other people—people who didn't write songs, people who didn't spend their twenties in basements and rehearsal spaces where the air tasted like sweat and ambition. I thought music was an escape route built out of chords.

Now, sometimes, I wonder if I just built a more complicated cage.

The tiny house fantasy returns, uninvited and insistent. It's not the house itself. It's the idea that a life could be small enough to hold.

Touring teaches you a particular kind of math: how to measure your worth in mile markers, in door counts, in tips, in streams, in the number of people who came up after the set and used the word *real*. You learn to smile when they tell you you're "authentic," because in this economy authenticity is just another genre.

I sit on the edge of the bed, notebook in my lap, and flip back a few pages. More fragments. More feverish attempts to trap something before it escapes. Every page looks like the inside of a mind arguing with itself.

There's a reason I keep the notebook. Not for the songs—for the proof.

Proof that I have been here. That I have tried. That I have made something out of all this motion.

Proof that I didn't spend my life only driving.

The phone buzzes suddenly. I jump, which is embarrassing. The screen lights.

A notification from a banking app:

A deposit posted.

I stare at it, waiting for it to become something else—for the amount to grow out of shame and into dignity.

It's not nothing. It's also not enough.

Last night's pay, minus gas, minus the percentage that goes to the invisible costs: strings, repairs, the slow fraying of a body you keep asking to perform miracles. It's the kind of money that makes you understand why old musicians either become saints or cynics. There isn't much room in the margins for normal.

I get dressed and pack in the practiced order—shirt, jeans, socks, charger, notebook, guitar. Everything has its place because if it doesn't, the whole life starts to feel like it could blow away in the wind.

Outside, the air is sharp. Winter has teeth. My breath comes out in pale bursts that vanish quickly, like applause.

In the lot, the blue Chevy G20 sits under a streetlight that flickers like it's tired of illumination. We bought it used—late model, decent miles—then turned it into a moving compromise: a plywood sleep platform, storage bins strapped down like cargo, a small power setup that keeps our phones and a lamp alive. Between hotel stays, that van is our home in the way a lifeboat is a home: you live there because you must.

Sam is already in the driver's seat, hood up, nursing coffee like it's medicine. Sam Rourke—my childhood friend, my counterweight, the guy who can look at me mid-spiral and pull me back with one raised eyebrow. We grew up close enough to smell the same ocean, learned our first chords in the same damp Rhode Island air, and somehow never killed each other—an achievement that feels more impressive than any streaming number.

"You ready?" he asks.

"Yeah," I say. "You?"

Sam makes a sound that could be agreement or resignation.

"Always."

I load my gear carefully. Two acoustic cases. A small bag of cables. If the venue has a piano, Sam will use it for a song or two. Otherwise it's us—wood and wire and voice—stripped down enough that there's nowhere to hide.

Sam watches me shut the van door. "You okay?" he asks, because he knows the real question.

I consider lying for half a second, out of habit. Then I decide not to give him the cheap version of me.

"I got a text," I say.

His eyes sharpen. "Good text or bad text?"

"'Maybe' text."

Sam nods like a man hearing a weather report.

"Ah. The classic."

I slide into the passenger seat and pull the notebook out one more time. I turn to a clean page, because I'm superstitious in the other direction too. If I don't write something in the morning, the day will swallow me whole.

I write the lyric cleanly this time, like I'm trying to make it respectable:

I want to live in a tiny house
with a few good books
and this old six-string.

Then, underneath, I add the line I found on the flyer, as if I'm making a contract with myself:

I'm trying to run away from the status quo.

TRACK 01 — TINY HOUSE THEORY

I stare at the words. They don't fix anything. They also don't lie.

Sam turns the key. The G20 coughs, catches. The heater begins to push out air that's only slightly less cruel than the outside.

My phone buzzes again.

A message from an unsaved number—the kind of number that can rearrange your week with four words.

Heard good things about last night.
Small showcase next month.
Might be a good room.
You around?

My heart does the stupid thing it always does: it jumps.

I hate that. I hate how quickly hope can take over the body—how it arrives like a drug you didn't remember you were addicted to.

Sam glances over.

"That the 'maybe'?"

I show him the screen. He reads it, then looks forward again, face neutral.

"Well," he says, "if the room's good, at least the chairs can watch us suffer in comfort."

I laugh—quiet, involuntary. Not joy, exactly. More like recognition.

This is how it works. This is the touring musician's weather: a sudden patch of sun on the highway, a hint of spectrum, then the cloud moving in again.

I type back before I can overthink it.

Yeah. I'm around.

Then I put the phone down, as if it might burn me.

The van pulls out of the lot and onto the road, tires making that steady sound that becomes your second heartbeat when you live like this.

I glance at the notebook one more time, at the tiny house lines sitting there like a prayer I'm not sure I believe.

THE QUIET PARTS

The status quo waits in every direction, patient as gravity. And still—still—we drive.

Track 02 — Halo

When you wake up, do you feel you were wrong?
Are you fighting with your mind, or with the wall?
I can tell when you wake—
your halo is split in half as well.
A candle sits on your favorite book.
Wax runs down like blame.
You took the bad and gave it a face.

By the time the sun shows up, we're already moving.

Touring turns mornings into a kind of forced amnesia: you wake, you gather your pieces, you leave. You don't linger, because lingering invites questions, and questions are expensive. On the road, the only thing that's reliably affordable is momentum.

The blue Chevy G20 is warm only in the way a body is warm after a fever—heat that doesn't comfort, just proves you survived the night. The plywood platform in the back is piled with blankets and instrument cases. There's a small lamp clipped near the ceiling that we use when we're sleeping in parking lots, but right now the van is running and the lamp is off. Daylight, such as it is, leaks through the windows in a dull, indifferent wash.

Sam drives. I watch the highway unspool and try not to check my phone like it's a pulse.

The "good room" text from yesterday sits in my messages, bright as a bruise. I told myself I'd answer later—after coffee, after a shower, after I felt like a person instead of a traveling wound.

But later is a myth. Later is what you tell yourself when you're afraid of the yes.

Sam glances over.

"You gonna do it?"

"I already did," I admit.

His mouth twitches.

"Of course you did."

Outside, the world is winter and asphalt and the occasional glimpse of water between trees. We pass towns that look identical from the highway: chain restaurants, gas stations, low buildings with flags out front, parking lots salted into ugly.

I open my camera roll and scroll past the last few nights: posters, blurry stage shots, a picture Sam took of the van parked under a streetlight—blue paint catching a little halo of illumination, like it was trying to look holy.

A new clip appears. Someone tagged us overnight.

It's from last night's set—grainy, loud, filmed from too close. You can hear my voice, thinner than it felt onstage, threaded through the room's chatter. For a few seconds it's almost flattering: the small cheer at the end of the chorus, the way the room seems to lean in.

Then I make the mistake of reading the comments. At first, they're fine.

This is sick.

What song is this?

Dude's got a voice.

Then the other kind arrive, like a tide turning.

Who is this?

Try hard.

TRACK 02 — HALO

Cringe.
Bro looks like he sleeps in his car.

I swallow, jaw tight. The worst part isn't the insult. The worst part is that it lands near something already tender: the knowledge that we do, sometimes, sleep in our car.

Sam notices my face shift.

"Don't do that to yourself," he says.

"What?"

"Reading strangers like they're priests," he replies. "They're just bored. Bored people get noisy."

I lock the phone and turn it face-down. My chest stays tight anyway.

A halo isn't a moral thing. It isn't holiness. It's the version of yourself you carry into rooms so the room doesn't have to deal with your need. It's the polite smile, the grateful tone, the practiced humility. It's the armor you call charm.

And the problem with armor is that you start believing it's your skin.

We stop at a service plaza around ten. The air outside is brutal and clean. Cold punches the last of sleep from my face. I stand near the van while Sam goes inside for coffee, and I stare at the G20 like it's a mirror I can't stop using.

We retrofitted the thing ourselves. Hardware-store plywood. A cheap foam mattress cut to size. Storage bins labeled with tape: STRINGS, CABLES, MERCH. It's not glamorous, but it's ours. A small movable life.

I should be grateful for that.

Sometimes gratitude is just another costume.

My phone buzzes again. This time it's Zoey.

Zoey doesn't do long texts. She does efficient love. She's learned that if she lets herself spill too much onto a screen, the screen doesn't hold it—it just makes her feel foolish later.

Her message is three lines:

Drive safe.
How was last night?
Call me when you can.

I stare at it until my throat tightens. Zoey always says *drive safe* like the road is a jealous god.

Sam returns with coffee and hands me one without asking.

"Your Ocean State queen?" he asks, gentle.

I nod.

"You gonna call her?"

"After we get settled," I say, which is the touring version of soon.

Sam doesn't argue. He just sips his coffee and looks out at the highway like he's watching weather.

Back in the van, we drive toward the next room. The next stage. The next small circle of light.

By late afternoon, we pull up behind a venue that smells like old brick and frying oil. Inside, the stage is low and the sound system is decent. There's a piano in the corner, dusted but intact, like someone once believed in elegance here.

Sam points at it.

"We doing the sad one?"

I laugh once.

"If it's in tune."

He walks over and taps a key. The note rings out clean enough.

"Miracles," he says.

Soundcheck is simple with a duo. Two acoustics. Two mics. A DI. When we play stripped, there's no place to hide—no wall of sound to lean on, no drummer to carry adrenaline. The song is either alive or it isn't.

The room starts filling around seven. A couple at the bar. A small cluster near the stage. A woman alone with a notebook. Men in work boots with tired eyes. People who came because they wanted the night to mean something without costing too much.

That's my favorite kind of crowd. The ones who still believe in small stakes.

We go on at nine.

The lights are warm and a little too close. Heat rises. My hands settle on the guitar neck. Sam's right hand keeps time beside me like a quiet heart.

For the first two songs, everything works. Not fireworks—something steadier. The room listens. The air holds still. A chorus lands and stays landed.

Between songs, I thank them. I make a small joke about the drive. They laugh in the right places, and for a moment I feel almost human.

Then I catch my reflection in a dark window near the bar—face lit from below, eyes tired, the outline of my head circled by stage light.

Halo.

The word hits like a cue. The lyric I wrote months ago—half accusation, half warning—slides up from wherever it's been sleeping inside me.

Are you fighting with your mind, or with the wall?

I sing the next verse and feel my voice tighten. Not from strain—from truth. The song isn't just leaving my mouth; it's pulling something out with it.

Halfway through the set, my phone buzzes in my pocket. I ignore it. I'm learning to ignore the world when the room is giving me something. But the buzz happens again, longer this time.

Sam looks at me, eyebrows raised, question in his face.

I shake my head. Not now.

We finish the set. Applause. Real, not huge. The kind that feels like a hand on the back.

After, in the small quiet behind the stage, I check my phone.

A new comment thread on the clip. More noise. More strangers.

More opinions.

And one message from Zoey:

You okay?

Two words. The simplest question. The hardest one.

I type back:

Yeah. Just tired. We played well. Miss you.

It's true and it's not enough, which is how most of my truths have started to feel.

Sam pulls two waters from the cooler and hands me one.

"Don't chase ghosts," he says.

"What?"

"Online," he says. "Those people don't get a vote."

I nod, but my body doesn't believe him. My body keeps reacting like every opinion is a verdict.

Later, after load-out, we sit in the van for a minute before turning the key. The parking lot lights flicker. Cold air seeps in around the door seals.

The day's adrenaline drains out of me the way it always does—fast, unforgiving.

In the quiet, the last line arrives like a diagnosis.

When you wake up, you're washed in gray.

Sam starts the engine. The G20 coughs, catches. The headlights carve a tunnel through the dark.

We pull onto the road again, chasing the next room, carrying our little cracked halos with us—half light, half burden—still hanging on, still threatening to fall.

Track 03 — Number Three

I have learned the math of being chosen last.
A quiet third place, a hand kept waiting.
When the door closes on the others, will you turn?
Will you call what is left of me enough?
If you enter my mind, will you survive it—
or will you leave me numbered again?

There are certain truths you learn the way you learn a chord: badly at first, then by repetition, then by pain.

One of mine is that success has a waiting room, and I've lived in it for years. Not the glamorous waiting room—the one with bottled water and soft chairs and somebody calling your name like it's inevitable. Mine is the kind with flickering lights and stale carpet. The kind where you hear the door open for someone else every so often and still convince yourself you're next.

On paper, our tour looks like progress. That's how it's designed. Cities in a neat list. Dates aligned like purpose. A photo every night with a different wall behind it, a different bar logo, a different batch of strangers lifting their phones as if recording is the same as loving.

In reality, it's a loop. You drive, you play, you sleep, you drive again. Sometimes the room is packed. Sometimes it's three tired people and a bartender who can't remember your name. Either way, you learn the job: make someone feel something and then, politely, leave them behind.

The blue Chevy G20 eats miles like it was built for hunger. Sam calls it "the whale," because it's big enough to swallow a life. I call it "home" when I'm lying to myself, and "vehicle" when I'm trying to be honest. in the back is the plywood platform we built, the storage bins, the little lamp. Between hotel stays, it's where we stretch out our bodies and pretend this is temporary.

Sam drives through a hard gray morning while I stare at my phone like it's a confession booth.

A message from Kate sits at the top of my screen. I didn't save her contact the first time—superstition, maybe. Like naming something makes it real, and real things can disappoint you.

Now her name is there anyway. Kate. Four letters that feel like a door handle.

She texts the way industry people text: breezy, efficient, never too warm, as if warmth is a form of liability.

Heard good things about last night.
Showcase lineup is shifting.
Could be a slot next month.
You around?

Could. Slot. Next month. Words designed to keep you available.

Sam glances over.

"Kate again?"

"You remembered her name?"

"I remember the way you looked when you read it," he says. "Same look you had in ninth grade when Coach Rizzo said you might start."

I laugh once—sharp. The laugh doesn't fix the ache.

I type back something careful, something that doesn't sound like I'm kneeling:

Yeah. We're around.

TRACK 03 — NUMBER THREE

Then I sit there with the phone in my hand and feel the familiar ache rise in my chest: the ache of being kept on standby.

Number three is a strange place to live. You're close enough to taste it, not close enough to touch. You get the benefits without the permanence: a little attention, a little money, a little validation. Just enough to keep you moving. Not enough to let you stop.

At noon we stop for gas, and the number on the pump climbs like a dare. Sam swipes his card, jaw tight.

"Another holy offering," he says.

"We'll make it back," I tell him.

He gives me a look.

"We always make it back. That's the problem."

On the drive, Sam tells me about a kid we grew up with in Rhode Island—a guy who used to play basement shows in Pawtucket and now sells insurance in Warwick, married, two kids, a lawn that looks like it's been combed.

"He seems happy," Sam says, voice neutral.

"Does he?" I ask.

"Happy enough," Sam replies. Then, quieter: "Sometimes I wonder what happy enough feels like."

I don't answer. Because I wonder too, and saying it out loud feels like betrayal.

That night we're opening for a bigger act in a room that actually has a stage. Real lights. A sound tech who looks like he's been doing this longer than I've been alive. The kind of venue where you can imagine, for a minute, that this is a rung and not the same loop with a nicer logo.

We load in early because the promoter asked us to, and because we're still the kind of duo that arrives early, as if punctuality might be mistaken for inevitability.

Backstage, the headliner's crew moves like they've been promised something. Their cases are cleaner. Their schedule is printed. Their confidence has an odor—not arrogance exactly, just the faint cologne of being caught by the right current.

Sam watches them for a second, then leans toward me.

"Must be nice," he murmurs.

"Don't," I say.

"I'm not," he replies. "I'm observing."

Observation is how Sam survives. I survive by pretending.

We do a quick soundcheck. Two mics. Two acoustics. A DI. No wall of sound to hide behind. If the song fails, it fails in plain daylight.

The promoter pulls me aside.

"Thirty minutes. Hit your best stuff. The crowd's here for the other guys."

He says it like we're an appetizer.

"Got it," I say, because what else do you say?

We go on at eight.

The room is already half full, bodies angled toward the bar, toward each other, toward the promise of the main event. A few people look up when we step onto the stage, polite curiosity in their faces.

I grip the mic and smile—the practiced smile, the one that makes strangers feel like friends and makes me feel like a liar.

"Hey," I say. "Thanks for coming out early."

Sam's guitar comes in beside mine—steady, clean, the rhythm of a guy who knows how to keep me from running away mid-song.

The first song lands politely. The second lands a little better. By the third, a few heads nod in time. A few people drift closer, as if they've decided to give us a chance.

Halfway through the set, I catch a woman in the front row actually listening. Not filming. Not chatting. Listening with her face open, like she's letting the sound do its work.

It hits me like a small mercy.

TRACK 03 — NUMBER THREE

I sing harder—not louder, just more honest. The room tightens. The air holds.

When we finish, the applause is real. Not huge, but real. A handful of people clap like they mean it, not like they're waiting for permission.

Backstage, Sam wipes his hands on his jeans and lets out a slow breath.

"See?" he says. "Not nothing."

"Not nothing," I agree, and the phrase feels like both comfort and sentence.

While the headliner sets up, we stand near our cases and watch the machinery of someone else's success assemble itself. Their soundcheck is louder, more assured. Their tour manager speaks into a headset like the night is a controlled operation, not a gamble.

A photographer snaps a few shots of them without asking.

Nobody asks to take pictures of us.

That's fine, I tell myself. It's fine.

Later, after the headliner finishes and the crowd spills out into the cold, we stand by our small merch table. Two piles of shirts. A handwritten sign. A jar for tips that looks like it's ashamed of itself.

A guy buys a shirt and tells me we sounded "tight," which is a funny compliment for two people with acoustic guitars. A woman asks if we're on Spotify. A kid wants a sticker.

And then someone says it—the compliment that is both blessing and bruise:

"Man, you should be bigger."

"Thanks," I say, and I mean it, and I hate it.

Because *bigger* is what people say when they want to praise you without having to do anything to help. Bigger is what the world promises you right before it walks away.

We pack up fast because openers don't get to linger. Outside, the G20 waits under a streetlight, blue paint catching the halo like a joke.

In the driver's seat, Sam starts the engine and glances at me.
"You gonna write about it?"
"About what?"
He shrugs.
"Being close. Being invisible. Being... you."
I pull my notebook out because I don't know what else to do with the feeling. The page is blank and hungry.
I write:
You know I've been your number three.
Then, underneath, as if I'm addressing a person instead of an idea:
The next time it's over, will you come to me?
I stop. I look at it. It reads like I'm talking to Kate. Like I'm talking to Zoey. Like I'm talking to the door itself—the one that keeps opening for other people.
Or maybe I'm talking to the part of myself that keeps waiting for permission to begin.
Sam pulls us onto the highway. The van hums. The road opens up like a long sentence I'm doomed to keep finishing.
Number three, once again, goes on the road—numbered again.

Track 04 — Why Am I Not the One

I have offered miracles like loose change.
I have crossed walls that should have stopped a body.
I have worn every mask that fit your hunger.
Still, you do not name me.
So I will not become the world to be held by you.
I will break clean in my own hands.

There's a particular kind of exhaustion that doesn't come from lack of sleep. It comes from being awake—truly awake—to the fact that you're doing everything you were told to do, and the universe is still acting like it didn't hear you.

We drive four hours after the opener gig, chasing the next date like it owes us something. The blue Chevy G20 becomes its own planet: stale air, buzzing chargers, a nest of cables, crumbs in the cup holders. The little lamp above the sleep platform rattles with every crack in the road, like it wants to be useful and can't.

Sam drives with both hands on the wheel, steady as a metronome. I keep replaying the night in my head—not because it was terrible, but because it was close.

Close is worse than bad.

Bad nights are clean. Bad nights are obvious. You can blame the sound, the weather, the wrong song order, the guy at the bar who kept yelling requests like the stage was a jukebox. Bad nights give you a reason.

Close nights don't. Close nights feel like you've been shown a doorway and then, politely, the door has been shut again. Not slammed. Not locked. Just closed—like someone doesn't want to be rude.

We're in a motel by midnight. The room smells like bleach and old fabric. I lie on top of the comforter and stare at the ceiling while Sam showers, the water thudding against the wall like a quiet argument.

My phone rests on my chest like a weight. Every few minutes I lift it, check it, set it down again, as if repetition could manufacture a message.

Nothing.

I should stop doing that. I know I should. But the part of me that wants the break doesn't understand *should*. It understands dopamine. It understands anticipation. It understands the exquisite torture of maybe.

At 2:14 a.m., I open the Notes app and type what I won't say out loud.

Why am I not the one?

I stare at it until it starts looking like a foreign language.

There's a childishness to the question that makes me hate myself. Like I'm owed something. Like I'm the center of the story and the plot is malfunctioning.

But it isn't entitlement.

It's bewilderment.

Because I've watched people with less craft—less hunger, less care—stumble into rooms that change their lives. I've watched them catch the right eye at the right time and rocket forward with the kind of speed that makes you start believing in fate.

And I've watched people with everything fade out quietly, like a song you loved that stops getting played.

TRACK 04 — WHY AM I NOT THE ONE

The randomness is what gets you. The randomness makes you superstitious.

It makes you start looking for patterns where there are none. It makes you start believing in weird little rituals: the right boots, the right guitar pick, the right caption, the right city to write in. It makes you bargain with the universe like the universe is a promoter you can charm.

I type a second line.

I could be anything and still not be the one.

That one hurts because it's true.

I could change my hair. I could change my sound. I could write cleaner hooks, simpler choruses—songs that smile for the algorithm. I could talk more onstage. I could talk less. I could be mysterious. I could be loud. I could be a brand.

And still, the door might not open.

In the morning, Sam is already outside loading the G20. He moves quietly, efficiently, like a man who respects the physics of fatigue. The sky is the color of dirty dishwater. Winter doesn't do sentiment.

"Coffee?" he asks, holding out a cup.

I take it and let the heat sting my fingers. "Thanks."

He watches me for a moment. "You sleep?"

"Not really."

He nods like that's the expected answer. "You wanna talk about it?"

I almost lie. Habit reaches for *fine* like it's a life raft.

Instead, I shrug. "I'm just... stuck."

Sam doesn't push. He never pushes. He's been my counterweight since we were kids—since Providence was still the whole world and we thought a song could solve anything.

We get on the highway.

My phone buzzes.

My body reacts before my mind can manage it—hope and dread

arriving in the same pulse.

It's an email.

Subject: Re: Showcase?

My heart lurches.

Then I open it and the lurch turns into a slow fall.

It's from Kate. Four sentences. Three of them are polite.

Hey—sorry for the delay.

The lineup shifted and we had to make changes.

Love what you're doing—let's keep in touch.

I'll reach out if something opens up.

Let's keep in touch.

The musician's funeral phrase.

I stare at the screen until the words feel like static. Behind the glass, the road keeps moving. Sam keeps driving. The world continues, indifferent to my private collapse.

I close the email and set my phone face-down like it's contagious.

Sam glances over without taking his eyes off the lane. "That a no?"

"It's a 'maybe later,'" I say.

He makes a sound that is almost a laugh. "So... a no."

We drive another hour. At a gas station, I go inside for water and stand behind a man in a suit buying lottery tickets. He scratches one right there at the counter. He wins twenty dollars. The clerk smiles like they've both performed a small miracle.

I watch it happen and feel something ugly rise in my chest: envy, absurd and immediate. Not of the money.

Of the luck.

Back in the van, Sam asks, "You good?"

I answer automatically. "Yeah."

Fine again. Fine everywhere. Fine as a shared language for people who don't want to start a fire while they're still trapped in the same vehicle.

TRACK 04 — WHY AM I NOT THE ONE

My phone buzzes again.

Zoey.

I hesitate before answering because I can already hear her tiredness through the screen, the way you can hear weather before you open the door.

I call.

She picks up on the second ring. "Hey," she says.

"Hey," I reply. "You okay?"

A pause. "I'm... fine."

Fine. The word follows me like exhaust.

"What's wrong?" I ask.

"I don't know," she says, and the honesty in it breaks something open. "I'm just... tired, Jude."

"I'm tired too," I say.

"I know," Zoey replies. And there's tenderness in it. Real tenderness. "But you're tired out there. Then you come home tired. Then you leave again. And I'm always—" She stops, searching. "I'm always bracing."

Bracing. Like she's waiting for impact.

I grip the phone harder, as if pressure could change what's true. "I'm trying," I say.

"I know you are," Zoey says. "But trying isn't the same as being here."

The highway noise fills the gap between us. Tires on pavement. Wind against glass. The sound of absence as a steady, practical thing.

"What do you want me to do?" I ask, and I hate the question because it sounds like surrender.

Zoey exhales. "I want you to stop asking me to understand something that keeps hurting me."

I close my eyes. I can see her house—the one full of my things and not me. I can see the places where my absence has become furniture.

"I love you," I say.

"I love you too," she answers. "But I can't keep holding this forever."

Forever. Another word that turns into a threat when you're not careful.

"I'm coming home after this run," I say. "For real."

Silence.

Then, softly: "You always say soon."

"I know," I whisper.

"Okay," she says, and the okay is gentle and devastating. "Be careful out there."

"Yeah—be safe," I say, the old reflex rising anyway.

The call ends.

Sam doesn't ask what she said. He just keeps driving, which is its own kindness.

Track 05 — Inkwell

I only write when I am wrong.
From my heart to the bone.
My heart explodes.
The inkwell in my throat has set the tone.
Metal strikes the page and my thoughts are excused.
Blood thumps the paper.
Ink-poison in me.

The next show is in a town that feels like it was built to be passed through.

We arrive in late afternoon, the sky low and sullen—the kind of gray that makes even "day" feel like a technicality. The venue is tucked between a shuttered storefront and a tire shop, a brick rectangle with a neon sign that hums like a tired insect. The poster on the door has my name in bold, the letters trying to do the heavy lifting of significance:

MILES SKYE (with Sam Rourke)

Inside, the room is empty except for the bartender and a sound tech who doesn't look up when we walk in. It smells like beer and bleach and something old—the ghost of a hundred nights that mattered intensely to somebody and then vanished.

Sam and I unload in silence. We're both functioning. We're both fine. We're both good at being fine.

Out back, the blue Chevy G20 waits—platform, bins, blankets, our whole small life packed tight—ready to swallow another night.

During soundcheck, I sing a few lines just to make sure my voice is still mine.

It comes out clean enough. The monitors give it back slightly altered—like a version of me with the sharp edges filed down. The sound tech nods once, which is basically a standing ovation in sound-tech language.

Sam runs a few chords on his acoustic, then looks around the room like he's scanning for furniture in a new apartment. In the corner sits an upright piano, dusty but intact.

"Is that real?" he asks.

I walk over and press a key. The note rings out thin but true.

"Real enough," I say.

Sam smiles. "We can do the bridge on that one."

There's time to kill. There's always time to kill.

Sam disappears outside to smoke and make a phone call he'll pretend isn't about money. The bartender wipes the same spot on the bar twice, bored in the way only a weekday can make you bored. The sound tech scrolls his phone like he's waiting for a better life to arrive.

I drift toward the back of the room where the light is dimmer, where nobody expects me to be charming. My notebook is in my jacket pocket. I can feel it like an extra organ.

Songwriting doesn't respect your schedule. It doesn't care if you're tired or busy or trying to be normal. It arrives when it wants to arrive, and if you don't catch it, it turns into an itch that lives under your skin.

I sit on a stool near the back wall and pull the notebook out.

The pages are swollen from humidity and use. There's a coffee stain that looks like a continent. The cover is frayed, corners chewed the way anxiety chews on a person. I flip through, catching flashes of myself at different ages—different voices, different levels of certainty.

TRACK 05 — INKWELL

Some lines are good. Some lines are crimes. Some are so earnest they make me want to apologize to the universe.

Even the bad ones have value. They prove I was trying.

I stop on the page that's been haunting me.

The inkwell in my throat has set the tone.

I read it again. Then again. I can almost feel it—something dark lodged behind my tongue, a reservoir of language that tastes like metal and want.

The most seductive lie about music is that it's pure expression—that it's just you, pouring your heart into the world, and the world receiving it like a gift.

The truth is messier. Music is also extraction. You dig something out of yourself and you sell it, night after night, and the digging doesn't stop just because the audience claps. Sometimes the clapping makes you dig deeper.

I turn the page.

Blood thumps the paper.

Ink-poison in me.

I don't know why I keep returning to blood. I'm not violent. I'm not dramatic in the way people imagine artists are dramatic. I'm actually—if you ask Sam—painfully practical. I pay what I can. I track the mileage. I schedule the oil changes. I keep the van from turning into a coffin.

But when I write, something in me becomes less civilized.

When I write, I stop pretending there's an easy separation between what I feel and what I am.

Behind the bar, the bartender turns on a playlist. A song I recognize slips through the speakers—one of those artists who "made it," whose voice is now a kind of public property. The mix is perfect. The chorus is built like architecture.

I feel the old resentment rise—hot and immediate—followed by shame for feeling it at all.

I don't resent *them*, not really. I resent the randomness that anoints one throat and not another. I resent how the world can hear hunger in one voice and call it destiny, and hear the same hunger in another voice and call it noise.

My phone buzzes.

A text from Kate.

I hesitate before opening it, like the screen might bite.

The slot's basically full.

You're still on my list, though.

Next time.

I appreciate your flexibility.

Next time.

It lands like a small slap.

I stare at the message until the letters soften at the edges. I can feel my body trying to turn disappointment into something useful—anger, fuel, a new verse. But disappointment is lazy. It just sits there.

Sam comes back in, cold air clinging to his hoodie. He sees my face and doesn't ask for details.

"Next time," he says, like he can read it off my skin.

"Yeah," I reply.

He nudges the piano bench with his foot. "Cool. Then we'll do the bridge extra sad for the ten people who show up."

I laugh—because he's funny, and because if I don't laugh I'll start believing the silence has meaning.

I flip to a clean page and write the date, the city, the venue name. I do this sometimes as if I'm keeping records for a future historian. As if anyone will ever need to know where the songs were born.

Then I write the first line that comes, without censoring it:

No one ever hears the things that I'm screaming out.

It's dramatic. It's also true—or, at least, it feels true in this room:

TRACK 05 — INKWELL

quiet bar, empty chairs, my voice bouncing off the walls like it can't find a place to land.

I scratch it out, not because it's wrong, but because it's too raw. Too much like pleading.

Underneath, I write:

Flush a melody.

The phrase feels like a command and a confession. Like the songs aren't only gifts—they're toxins I have to get out of me before they rot. Like if I stop writing, the whole system backs up.

Sam calls from the stage. "Doors in thirty."

We go into performance mode.

That shift—private to public—is so practiced it's almost automatic. I change my shirt. I wipe my hands. I tune the guitar. Sam checks the piano again, then sets his acoustic on its stand like he's putting a tool down before work.

People start coming in slowly. A couple at the bar. Three guys in work boots. A woman alone with a book. Two college kids whispering like they don't want to admit they're excited. The room fills to maybe forty—enough to feel alive, not enough to feel like an omen.

I watch them through the crack in the curtain and feel that familiar tightening in my chest.

This is the moment I always try not to romanticize: the few minutes before the first chord, when anything is still possible. When the room hasn't decided what it thinks of you. When you can still imagine, stupidly, that tonight might be the night someone sees you and calls it fate.

I hate that part of me. I also depend on it.

We walk onstage.

The lights hit my face. The room becomes a sea of dark shapes and attentive silence. My hands find the guitar the way they always do—muscle memory, devotion.

"Hey," I say into the mic, voice steady. "Thanks for coming out."

Polite. Professional. A man who is not, under any circumstances, needy.

We start the first song.

Sam falls in beside me—clean rhythm, quiet intelligence. He plays like a man who understands space, like he knows the silence between chords is part of the deal. The sound is good. The room listens. And for a few minutes I can almost forget Kate's text, the waiting room, the lottery-ticket luck of other lives.

This is the drug: the moment when the song becomes bigger than the person carrying it.

Halfway through the set, Sam crosses to the piano. He sits, cracks his knuckles once, and drops into the bridge like he's always lived inside keys. The room shifts. People look up. The piano changes the air. It makes the song feel older than us.

And in that bridge, I feel the words rise in my throat—an unplanned turn, a new line. It happens sometimes, when the room is right, when I'm tired enough to stop being careful.

I lean into the mic and let it out.

The inkwell in my throat has set the tone.

It's not polished. It's not perfect. But it's alive.

When the song ends, the applause is real. Not huge, but real. Hands clapping, bodies responding, the room acknowledging that something happened between us.

For a second, warmth moves through me—small, clean.

Then the warmth recedes, and what's left is the familiar hollow: the knowledge that the room will empty, the gear will be packed, the highway will swallow us again, and tomorrow morning I will wake up in another anonymous bed and check my phone like a man checking a pulse.

After the show, a few people come up to the merch table. Someone buys a shirt. Someone buys a sticker. Someone tells me they liked the "new line" in the middle of that one song.

"Which one?" I ask, careful not to sound too eager.

"The inkwell line," they say. "That was… I don't know. It hit."

I smile, because I don't know what else to do with that kind of intimacy from a stranger.

"Thanks," I say. "I appreciate it."

They leave, and I stand there with the strange sensation of having been briefly understood.

Later, when the bar is closed and the G20 is packed and the winter air cuts through my jacket, I sit in the passenger seat and take the notebook out again.

My hands shake a little from adrenaline and cold.

I flip to the page where I wrote *Flush a melody*, and beneath it I add: *Tonight, it worked.*

Then I pause and write the line I don't want to write but have to, because the truth always arrives eventually:

It still didn't change anything.

Sam starts the engine. The van's heater whines to life like it's annoyed at being asked.

As we pull into the dark, the streetlights smear across the windshield. Somewhere inside my throat, the inkwell refills.

And because I'm still me—because hope is my cheapest habit—I keep carrying the poison like it's medicine.

Track 06 — Next to Nowhere

> *Playing all these shows next to nowhere,*
> *the crowd applauds.*
> *I wish you were here.*
> *There is no one here tonight that makes me feel alive.*
> *I need you by my side:*
> *the drums, the cheers, the clanging beer bottles,*
> *the sound of my fears.*

The van is a generous liar.

It tells you you're going somewhere, even when you're only circling. It tells you you're in motion, which feels like progress if you don't look too closely at where you've been. It lulls you with the hum of tires on highway and the illusion of forward momentum, and if you're tired enough—if you want it enough—you can mistake that hum for a future.

We don't have a bus. We have the blue Chevy G20, and calling it a bus is the kind of joke you make so the truth doesn't bruise as badly.

The G20's interior is a geography of our small life: blankets bunched like a storm on the plywood platform, a hoodie jammed behind a seat as a pillow, cables coiled like sleeping snakes. A cardboard box of merch slowly losing its corners. An empty bottle rolling on the floor with every turn, tapping out that soft plastic percussion that eventually becomes part of your brain.

Outside, the world is winter and asphalt. The sky is the color of a washed-out photograph. We pass exits for towns we won't enter—names that flash by like characters in a book I'll never read.

Some days, I can't remember where we are until I check the GPS. My life has become a long sequence of exits.

Sam drives. He always drives the first stretch, the one that requires the most patience. He's better at patience than I am. I'm built for ignition. He's built for endurance.

"You want to switch?" he asks after an hour.

"Not yet," I say, though my hands twitch like they want something to do besides haunt my own thoughts.

We stop at a service plaza around noon. Everyone shuffles out stiffly, bodies rearranging themselves into human shapes again. Sam heads straight for coffee and a bathroom that doesn't smell like regret. I wander, hands in pockets, and feel that quiet loneliness that only shows up when you're with the person who knows you best and still can't save you from yourself.

In the corner of the plaza there's a little seating area—plastic chairs, bolted tables, the kind of place designed to make you leave quickly. I sit anyway. My notebook is in my jacket, and so is the letter I started three nights ago and never finished.

I pull the folded page out carefully, like it might tear. The paper is creased, smudged, written on a night when my hand couldn't hold steady—tired, or cold, or both.

The first line stares up at me:

Playing all these shows next to nowhere.

I read it and tasted metal. It isn't poetic, really. It's just an honest complaint dressed up as lyric so it can survive being said.

Next to nowhere. That's the thing about touring at this level: you're always adjacent. Adjacent to the bigger room. Adjacent to the better slot. Adjacent to the life you thought music might buy you.

I keep reading.

Writing you letters from the bus...

We don't have a bus, I think again, and the correction makes me wince. Because the word *bus* isn't about the vehicle. It's about the fantasy: that this is a real career, a real machine, a real life with infrastructure. That the road isn't just two guys and a van and the daily gamble of being heard.

I haven't sent a real letter in years. Nobody does. But I keep writing them—on receipts, on the backs of setlists, on motel stationery—because there's something about ink that feels more serious than a text. A letter feels like proof you meant it. A letter feels like an act of faith.

Zoey used to love my letters. When we were younger—when Benefit Street still felt like our center of gravity—I'd leave her notes in coat pockets, in book pages, on the dashboard of her car. She kept them in a shoebox like they were talismans. Weeks later she'd quote lines back to me, smiling, as if the words had become part of our private language.

Now I don't even know if she wants them.

Now everything feels like it has to be negotiated: time, attention, intimacy. The road turned love into a logistics problem.

I flip the page over, creases multiplying.

Frantic. Panicked. Homesick.

I can hear my own voice when I wrote it—pressed against a window somewhere, watching dark blur past, feeling that low-grade panic like a fever you can't sweat out. Not the dramatic panic of a breakdown. The steady panic of realizing you're building a life out of absence.

My phone buzzes.

I ignore it. Then it buzzes again, longer.

Zoey.

My chest tightens before I even answer. I tap accept.

"Hey," I say.

Her voice is small through the speaker, like it's coming from far away. "Hey."

A pause. A silence full of weather.

"Where are you?" she asks.

I glance at the plaza sign, as if the name could tell her what it feels like. "On I-81," I say. "Somewhere between... everything."

She laughs softly—not because it's funny, because it's familiar. "That's... helpful."

"I'm sorry," I say. "I'll be in—" I check the schedule in my head. "—Scranton tonight. Then Ithaca. Then... northwest."

Another pause. I can hear something in the background on her end—maybe a TV, maybe dishes, maybe the small domestic sounds of a life that continues while I'm out here pretending my absence is temporary.

"How was last night?" she asks.

"It was good," I say automatically. "Decent crowd. Good sound."

"That's good," she replies. Polite. Professional. Like she's talking to a coworker. Like the part of her that used to be thrilled by road stories has been replaced by an exhausted accountant.

"What about you?" I ask. "How are you?"

She hesitates. "I'm... fine."

Fine again. Fine as a towel thrown over a mess.

"What's wrong?" I ask, even though I already know. Something is always wrong now. Not a catastrophe—just the slow structural damage of distance.

"It's nothing," she says quickly. Then, softer: "It's just... weird, Jude."

"Weird," I repeat.

"Yeah," she says. "I'm living in a house where your stuff exists, but you don't. And people ask about you like you're... like you're a story."

That stings because it's true. I've become a story. The boyfriend on tour. The singer chasing a break. The romantic myth of a man living for his music.

Nobody asks her what it's like to live with a myth.

"I'm coming home soon," I say, because that's the line I always use.

"Soon," she echoes, and I hear the exhaustion in it. "You always say soon."

"I know," I say. "I'm so close, though."

"I know you are," she replies, and for a second her voice warms with something like tenderness. Then it cools again. "I just… I don't know what we're doing anymore."

The plaza suddenly feels too loud. Someone laughs near the coffee counter. A child cries. A door whooshes open and shut. All of it feels like it's happening in another dimension.

"We're doing this," I say, stupidly. "We're… building something."

"Are we?" she asks. Not accusing—just genuinely unsure, which is worse. "Because it feels like you're building something out there, and I'm just… here."

I want to tell her she's wrong. I want to tell her she's the reason I'm doing any of it. I want to tell her that every show is a brick in a house I'm trying to build for us.

But I can't say it without hearing how flimsy it sounds.

"I miss you," I say instead—simple, true, the only safe thing.

"I miss you too," she says, and I believe her. That's the tragedy. We miss each other sincerely and still can't seem to live in the same life.

"I have to go," she says after a moment. "I'm at work."

"Okay," I say. "Text me later."

"Yeah," she says. Then, almost as an afterthought: "Drive safe."

"You too," I say, because my brain is broken.

She laughs a little, and then the call ends.

I sit there a long moment holding the dead phone, staring at the letter.

The letter isn't a love letter anymore. It's a record of distance. It's a receipt for a life I keep purchasing with my own absence.

I fold it and tuck it back into the notebook. I don't know if I'll ever send it. I don't know if sending it would fix anything. Sometimes letters are just another way of postponing the real conversation.

Back in the lot, Sam is leaning against the G20, sipping coffee, eyes narrowed against the wind.

"You talk to her?" he asks.

"Yeah."

He watches my face, careful. "How bad?"

I shrug. "Not bad. Just… tired."

Sam nods. "Tired is bad when it keeps repeating."

We pull back onto the highway. The van accelerates. The tires find the familiar hum. Motion resumes—generous and indifferent.

As the miles pass, the panic returns—low, constant. Not the dramatic panic of falling apart. The steady panic of realizing time is moving whether or not you're ready.

I open my notebook on my knee and write one more line under the existing lyric, smaller this time:

If I stop moving, I might finally hear myself.

Sam keeps driving.

And I keep writing letters I don't send, as if words alone could build a tiny home.

SIDE B — TERMS & LIGHT

Track 07 — VIP Black Gucci

They part the line and usher us inside.
Midnight VIP—clean and silent.
Lint-free black, dressed for the flash.
Pictures tonight: pretend to have a good time.
This is not what we came to see.
Not onstage—just whiskey on ice.
We sparkle and fade, for only us to notice.
We are our own spectators.

The invite arrives like a dare dressed as a favor.

It's not official enough to be flattering. Not casual enough to be meaningless. It has just the right tone—breezy, inside-baseball, vaguely urgent—to make you feel that saying no would be a kind of self-sabotage.

A friend-of-a-friend texts it while we're parked outside a diner somewhere in Connecticut, waiting for pancakes because we're pretending we're the kind of people who eat breakfast.

You in the city tonight?
Industry thing. Back room.
Come through. Good faces.
Might be worth it.

"Might be worth it" is the line that gets you. *Might* is the hook. *Worth it* is the myth.

Sam doesn't want to go. You can tell by how fast he says, "Nope."

I look up from my coffee. "Nope?"

He gestures with his fork at the van outside—the blue G20 sitting in the cold like a loyal mutt. "We've got a show tomorrow. We've got miles. We've got a gas gauge that hates us. Why would we go play dress-up for people who won't remember our names?"

He's right. That's what makes it difficult. If he were wrong, saying yes would be easy.

"It's not a performance," I say. "It's just... showing up."

"That's the performance," Sam replies. "That's the whole circus."

I stare at the message again. *Good faces. Back room. Worth it.*

A room full of door handles.

"Come with me," I say, and I hear the faint desperation in it. I hate myself for that sound.

Sam sighs the way a man sighs when he's already agreed and resents his own loyalty. "Fine," he says. "But if someone says 'synergy,' I'm leaving."

We drive in. The city is cold and bright and loud in that way that makes every small person feel like a temporary mistake. The G20 looks absurd next to the sleek cars—blue paint dulled by winter salt, our little home-on-wheels squeezed into a parking space like it's trying not to take up too much of the world.

Inside the bar, the lighting is low and warm, curated to make everyone look interesting. Music thumps under conversation. The air smells expensive—perfume, whiskey, confidence.

At the front, a woman with glossy hair checks names on a list. She pauses on mine—just long enough to sting—then finds it, smiles, and gestures us in as if granting visas.

Already, that familiar ring of possibility tries to settle over my head.

In the back room, people cluster in tight groups like molecules. They

TRACK 07 — VIP BLACK GUCCI

laugh at each other's jokes too quickly. They touch each other's arms too often. A photographer drifts through, hunting faces that will make someone's feed look like access.

There are artists here, technically. But it doesn't feel like a room of art. It feels like a room of commerce wearing art's jacket.

Sam leans toward me and murmurs, "Everyone here looks like they're about to sell me a subscription."

I almost laugh. Humor is how we keep from becoming merchandise.

Someone hands us drinks we didn't ask for. We take them because refusing feels like a social crime. The whiskey burns. I tell myself it's warmth.

Across the room, a man in a clean suit talks into a woman's ear like he's selling her something private. He laughs softly at his own lines, as if he's practiced sounding casual. She nods as if she's practiced being impressed.

"Gatekeeper," Sam whispers.

"Maybe," I whisper back.

The man notices us watching and lifts his glass in a polite half-toast—so small it almost feels generous.

I nod like I belong.

This is the performance no one buys a ticket for: the offstage theater of looking comfortable in rooms you'd never enter if the dream weren't dangling you by the throat.

A guy approaches us. Black turtleneck. Sneakers that look like they cost a month of my rent. He introduces himself as a "consultant," which means nothing and everything. He says he's "working with a few emerging acts," and his eyes keep sliding past my shoulder like he's scanning for someone more profitable.

He asks what we're working on.

"The road," I say. "Writing. Playing."

"Love that," he says. "Love the grind."

Then he asks the question everyone asks, the one that sounds friendly but isn't:

"So what's your story?"

My story.

I want to laugh. I want to say: I'm from Rhode Island. I play small rooms. I drive until my spine forgets how to be still. I miss my girlfriend. I'm tired. I'm hopeful in the way a man is hopeful when he can't afford not to be.

But I know what he means. He means: what's the angle? What's the pitch? What's the thing we can sell that isn't just music?

So I give him something shaped like a story. Independent. Working. Growing. "Authentic." I say a few lines that are true and a few lines that are strategic, and I hate myself for how easy it is.

He nods with intense interest. "Amazing," he says. "We love authenticity right now."

Authenticity right now. As if it's seasonal. As if it has an expiration date.

He asks for my Instagram. I give it. He follows me in front of my face like a blessing administered via thumb.

Then he drifts away, already scanning the room for the next person who might be worth his attention.

Sam watches him go. "We should start a band called Right Now," he says. "Just to cash in."

"Shut up," I whisper, smiling despite myself.

Near the back, a cluster of people is taking pictures. The photographer arranges them with the same care a man arranges a meal. Someone tilts their chin toward the light. Someone laughs on cue. Someone turns a shoulder like they've rehearsed it in a bathroom mirror.

They want pictures tonight. Pretend to have a good time.

The line repeats in my head like a chorus I didn't ask for.

TRACK 07 — VIP BLACK GUCCI

A woman approaches me—one of the few faces in the room that looks unvarnished. She doesn't look like she's trying to be photographed. She looks like she came because she actually likes music.

"Hi," she says. "You're Miles Skye, right?"

I blink. "Yeah."

"I saw you in Providence a while back," she says. "You were... really good."

The sincerity startles me. It slices through the room's polished bullshit like a clean blade. For a second, something honest happens in my chest.

"Thank you," I say, and mean it.

"You deserve more," she adds, earnest. "You're gonna pop."

Pop. Like a bubble. Like a quick bright burst that leaves dampness and air.

She asks for a picture.

Of course she does. This room runs on pictures. It's how proof is manufactured.

I step beside her. Sam hovers a few feet away, arms crossed, wearing the expression of a man watching his friend put his heart on layaway. The photographer snaps. I hold the practiced smile. My body automatically turns a few degrees toward the light.

In the flash, I feel a quiet dislocation—like I'm watching myself play a character named Miles Skye.

After the picture, she thanks me and disappears back into the crowd, probably already uploading the proof.

Sam leans in. "You okay?"

"Yeah," I lie.

He doesn't call me on it. He just says, "Let's get air."

Outside, the cold hits my face like truth. The city's noise is sharper, less curated. I breathe it in like I'm starving.

We stand near the G20. The van's blue paint catches a streetlight and, for a second, it looks almost glamorous. Then a gust of wind carries the smell of trash and exhaust, and the spell breaks.

"You get what you needed?" Sam asks.

"What did I need?" I say, too fast.

He watches me. "Hope," he says simply. "The little hit."

I want to argue. I want to insist I came for networking, for professionalism, for strategy.

But he's right.

I check my phone. A couple new followers. A like on a clip. A DM that says *fire* and nothing else.

Nothing that opens.

I stare at the screen until my eyes blur.

This is the cruel magic of these nights: they make you feel close without giving you anything solid to hold. You leave with contacts, follows, compliments shaped like predictions. You leave with the same life you had when you walked in—only now you've spent the night performing, and you didn't even get to sing.

Back in the motel room later, Sam is asleep within minutes—face turned toward the wall, body dropped into exhaustion like surrender.

I sit on the edge of the bed and take out my notebook.

I flip to a clean page and write, without thinking:

Rolling up as a midnight VIP.

Then I stop, because it's a lie. We weren't VIPs. We were possibilities—names on a list someone could cross off without consequence.

Underneath, I write:

They want pictures tonight. Pretend to have a good time.

Then, because I need to remind myself what we actually are when the lights are off, I write the truest line in the whole room:

We just play as two friends.

We don't want to be a fad.

Outside, the city continues. Somewhere, someone's career is being born. Somewhere, someone is posting proof.

In this room, in this quiet, I can feel that old ring of light shifting again—cracked, heavy, still clinging.

Tomorrow we drive.

Tomorrow we play.

And the night's glitter dries on my skin like residue, reminding me that pretending is its own kind of work.

Track 08 — Turn Around

There is a moment when hiding becomes a sermon,
when silence is its own stage.
Turn around—
not for their hunger, not for their praise.
Turn around because you are still here.
Because a face is a kind of truth.
Because the heart cannot be carried backward forever.

The morning after the industry night, I wake up with glitter in my blood and none on my hands.

That's how those rooms work: nothing you can hold, nothing you can pack. You leave with a couple new followers and the sensation that you stood near a train that never stopped. The body remembers proximity as possibility; the mind remembers emptiness as insult.

Sam is already awake in the motel room, sitting on the edge of his bed, lacing his boots like he's trying to anchor himself to the day. He looks over when I sit up.

"You good?" he asks.

It's the road's favorite question. It means: are you functional enough to keep going?

"I'm fine," I say, and the lie is automatic.

Sam snorts softly. "You should get that printed on a shirt."

TRACK 08 — TURN AROUND

We pack without talking much—not because we're mad, but because the morning has weight and we don't want to add language to it. Outside, winter bites. The blue Chevy G20 waits under a weak streetlight, dulled by salt and miles.

We load up. We drive.

The road resumes its steady hum—the true soundtrack of our lives. The heater takes its time getting warm. The sky is a flat gray lid. Exits slide past like towns in a book I'll never open.

I keep thinking about the party and how I wore my best version of myself like a costume. I keep thinking about the woman who asked for a picture, how quickly a moment becomes proof.

And I keep thinking about Kate.

I haven't heard from her since the last "next time," but my body keeps expecting the phone to glow. Keeps expecting the universe to finally say: *now*.

Around noon, it does.

A text from an unknown number—the kind of message that tightens your stomach before you even read it.

You around tonight?

Small showcase. Private-ish.

Listening room.

Kate asked me to reach out.

If you can do 20, it could be worth it.

Sam watches my face change.

"That her?" he asks.

"Not her," I say. "Someone... for her."

"Ah. Proxy hope."

He's not wrong. The industry loves intermediaries. It lets everyone keep their hands clean.

"What do you want to do?" Sam asks. He says it like a real question, not a test.

The G20 hits a bump and the lamp over the sleep platform rattles faintly—small, domestic. A reminder that we're living inside a vehicle and calling it a plan.

"I think we should do it," I say.

Sam's jaw works for a second. Then he nods once.

"Okay. Then we do it clean. Two acoustics. One piano if the room has one. No circus."

"No circus," I repeat, as if saying it can keep the circus away.

We adjust the route. We lose time. We gain the illusion of possibility.

By evening we pull up to the address: a converted black-box space on a side street that smells like wet pavement and old smoke. No sign, just a door and a man outside with a clipboard. Inside, the lighting is warm and deliberate.

Backstage is a narrow hallway with a curtain that doesn't quite reach the floor. Someone has taped schedules to the wall. The paper flutters when the door opens, like nervousness itself has airflow.

Sam sets our cases down and scans the room.

"This is either good," he murmurs, "or it's expensive disappointment."

"Could be both," I say.

People arrive—forty, maybe fifty. Not a bar crowd. A listening crowd. They sit upright, controlled, attention folded neatly into their laps.

In the second row, I see her.

Kate.

She isn't dressed flashy. That's what makes her feel untouchable. Hair pulled back. Face calm. Beside her sits a man in a blazer who keeps leaning in to say things close to her ear. She nods occasionally without smiling.

Gatekeeping as a quiet sport.

My stomach tightens.

Sam nudges me lightly.

"Don't stare," he whispers. "That's how you turn yourself into a dog

TRACK 08 — TURN AROUND

begging at the table."

I look away, embarrassed by my own hunger.

A stagehand pops his head in.

"Five minutes."

Sam and I stand. We do the small pre-show rituals that make us feel less like we're walking into a firing line: tune, check strings, wipe hands, breathe.

We line up in the wing.

The lights dim. The room hushes.

Then we step out.

The stage is low. The seats are close enough I can see eyes. The quiet feels expensive.

I grip the mic.

"Hi," I say. "Thanks for being here."

We start with the song that behaves when people actually listen—the one with the chorus that lands softly and stays landed. Sam's guitar comes in beside mine: clean rhythm, steady pulse, the childhood friend who knows how to keep me from sprinting into my own panic.

Halfway through the first song, something loosens. Not confidence—something closer to surrender. The body remembers the job: sing, mean it, don't apologize for existing.

When the song ends, the applause is restrained but real. Not a roar—neat clapping. People acknowledging effort.

We move into the second song, slower. The one Zoey used to ask for, back when we were young enough to mistake absence for romance. I don't announce that. I just sing it and let the weight stay unnamed.

In the second verse, I glance at Kate despite myself.

She's watching without expression—evaluating, not unkindly. A gaze that doesn't say yes or no, only: *prove it*.

My chest tightens.

Turn around, my mind insists—stop hiding inside the careful version of yourself.

I've been hiding for years, but not in darkness. In performance. In politeness. In the investable version of me.

And suddenly, on this stage, I can't stand the burial anymore.

On the bridge, a line comes out that isn't on any record. It wasn't planned. It wasn't rehearsed. It arrives raw—as close to speaking as singing can get.

Sam's head snaps toward me for half a second—tiny alarm, tiny admiration—then he keeps playing. That's what he does: he holds the structure while I risk the collapse.

The room changes. A hush inside the hush. Even the people who came to judge seem to lean in, just a fraction, as if the sound slipped past their defenses.

When the song ends, the applause is slower now. Heavier. Less polite.

We do one more—tight, clean, no rambling between songs. Twenty minutes means twenty minutes. We treat their attention like it costs something.

Then it's over.

We step offstage. The adrenaline drops. The hallway feels suddenly too small for my body.

Kate appears like she was always going to.

"Good," she says, with no gush in it. One syllable—controlled, professional. It hits harder than praise.

"Thank you," I manage.

She nods toward Sam. "Solid playing," she says, then looks back at me. "Do you have a live clip from tonight?"

"Someone recorded," I say. "I can get it."

"Get it," she says. "Send it. And send me your last release."

My mouth goes dry. "Okay."

She watches me for one more beat, then adds, "Don't sit on it. These

TRACK 08 — TURN AROUND

things move."

Then she's gone—already dissolving into conversation, already becoming rumor.

Sam appears beside me, eyebrows raised. "Was that... something?"

"I think so," I say, and hate how small it sounds.

Outside, the night is cold and honest. We load gear into the G20 in near silence, each movement precise. You don't celebrate on the road until the celebration can't be taken back.

In the van, Sam starts the engine. The heater groans.

He glances at me. "How do you feel?"

I consider the answer—private, not public.

"Like I turned around and saw the cliff," I say.

Sam smiles once.

"Yeah," he says. "But you didn't jump."

I look out at the streetlights smearing across the windshield.

Turning around implies there's something behind you you've been refusing to face. Something you've been outrunning.

Tonight, for a few minutes, I stopped running long enough to be seen.

Whether that's the beginning of a break or just another near-miss wearing better clothes, I can't tell.

But as we merge into traffic, I feel my cracked halo shift—lighter, maybe, or just differently weighted.

And for the first time in a long time, I let myself think that turning around isn't for the room at all—

it's for the life waiting at home.

Track 09 — Streetlight Secrets

We choose the hour that belongs to no one.
We choose the light that does not ask questions.
We take our names off the world for a moment—
and run
down the last stretch of dark,
until your face appears like a match
and the secret begins to breathe.

A secret is a kind of second life.

It isn't always a person. Sometimes it's a sentence you never repeat. Sometimes it's an email you keep rereading like scripture. Sometimes it's an opportunity that makes you behave like you've been promised something—before anything has been promised at all.

Two nights after the showcase, we're parked behind a motel off the highway, the blue Chevy G20 tucked between a dumpster and a line of quiet cars. The sign buzzes softly. The air smells like wet salt and gasoline—New England winter clinging to everything.

Sam is inside, showering. Through the thin wall I heard the muffled thud of water, the sound of a man trying to rinse the road off his skin. So, I went to sit in the van with the lamp turned low, notebook open on my knee, phone face-up like a dare.

Kate hasn't written again. That's the cruelty of her: just enough contact to wake your blood, then silence that forces you to do the imagining.

But I can't stop hearing her instruction—*Don't sit on it. These things move.*

For two days it's been grinding in my head like gears.

At 11:47, my phone lights up.

Unknown number.

My heart jumps the way it always does, trained to salute possibility before it checks for safety.

I answer too fast. "Hello?"

A pause. Then a voice I recognize—calm, unhurried.

"Miles. It's Kate."

The van suddenly feels too small for my body. I sit up straighter, as if posture can make me more legitimate.

"Hi," I say.

"Sorry it's late," she says. Not apologetic—just stating the weather. "I listened back to a clip from the room."

"Okay."

"You have a strong voice," she says, and this time the sentence carries weight. "And the way you two play—stripped—works. It reads."

Reads. Like I'm a text. Like the room is a page and my body is ink.

"Thank you," I say, and my throat feels dry.

She pauses, and in that pause I hear machinery: scheduling, names, rooms, the quiet shuffle of people being weighed.

"There's a small bill next month," she says. "Two dates. Real listening room. Not big money. But it's a real room, and there may be press."

My chest tightens.

"Yes. We can—"

"Hold," she says, gently. The gentleness doesn't soften it; it controls it. "I'm not offering it yet. I'm asking if you could commit if I do."

I swallow.

"Yes."

"Okay," she says. "Then here's the thing: if this happens, you keep it quiet. No posts. No teasing. No telling the world you're 'about to.'"

I glance out at the motel windows—thin curtains, sleeping shapes. The whole building feels like a conspiracy of ordinary lives.

"Why?" I ask, then regret it. You don't ask *why* in these rooms. You say *yes* and try not to sound grateful.

"Because," she says, even, "nothing is real until it's on paper, and paper moves slower than mouths."

She isn't wrong. I've watched rumors build careers and bury them.

"Okay," I say. "Of course."

"Good," she says—small approval, a pellet of possibility.

Then, almost casually: "Send me your masters and one live video. Tomorrow. Not next week. Tomorrow."

"Tomorrow," I repeat, like a vow.

"Great. Goodnight, Miles."

And the call ends.

The screen goes dark. The van's little light hums. My hands are trembling, as if my body can't decide whether this is adrenaline or fear.

We choose the hour that belongs to no one.

I wrote lines like that years ago as romance—like secrecy meant control. Like hiding was power.

Now I understand secrecy is fear in a nicer suit: fear of losing the thing before you ever have it.

Outside, a streetlight glows at the edge of the lot, flickering like it's tired of being faithful. I step out and walk toward it because I need air, and because the circle of light feels like somewhere the truth can stand without collapsing.

Cold bites my face. My breath fogs and disappears. Cars hiss past on the road beyond the motel, each one carrying its own anonymous life.

Under the streetlight, I stare at my phone.

TRACK 09 — STREETLIGHT SECRETS

I want to call Zoey.

Not because I'm proud. Because the moment something good might happen, I reach for her like a talisman—the proof that this life has a point beyond my own ego.

But Kate said keep it quiet. And the second I tell Zoey, it turns into a promise. One more promise—something she has to hold. And I've asked her to hold too much.

My thumb hovers over Zoey's name anyway.

Then I do the cowardly thing.

I text her instead.

Miss you. Long day. You okay?

It's true and it's not the truth. A small packet of affection meant to quiet guilt.

The reply comes quickly, as if she was waiting.

Miss you too. I'm okay. Call when you can.

Call.

The word lands like a request and a test.

I could call. I could tell her: Kate called. There might be dates. There might be movement. There might be a room that matters.

And I can already hear the other half of it—the part that makes me hesitate:

But you can't tell anyone.

And it might not happen.

And I might break your heart again by getting excited about air.

A secret is a second life.

And I'm starting to understand the danger: it doesn't stay separate. It leaks into your tone. It changes what you choose. It makes you lie without lying.

Behind me, the motel door opens. Sam steps out, hair damp, hoodie up against the cold. He sees me under the streetlight and walks over.

"Everything okay?" he asks.

I hold the phone up like evidence.

"Kate called."

Sam's eyebrows lift.

"And?"

I tell him: two dates, maybe. Press, maybe. Masters tomorrow. Keep it quiet.

He listens without reacting, which is one of the reasons he keeps me in balance. When the world throws glitter at me, he keeps his hands clean.

When I finish, he says, "So it's not a yes."

"It's… close," I say, hating the word as soon as it leaves my mouth.

Sam nods slowly.

"Okay. Then we do the work. We send the stuff. We keep it quiet."

I look at him.

"That's it?"

He shrugs.

"What else is there?"

I want there to be something else. I want him to tell me this is the beginning. I want him to say the universe finally blinked at us.

But Sam has never been sentimental about gates.

He watches my face.

"You gonna tell Zoey?"

The question lands in the center of my chest.

"I don't know," I admit.

Sam glances back at the motel, then at the van, then at me.

"Here's what I know," he says. "If you tell her, it becomes hope she has to carry. If it doesn't happen, she carries the fall too."

I swallow hard.

"And if I don't tell her?" I ask.

Sam's expression softens.

"Then you carry it alone. And that's when you start changing."

TRACK 09 — STREETLIGHT SECRETS

We stand under the streetlight in silence, the two of us framed like a photograph nobody will take.

I know how to turn my face toward rooms that might change my life. I know how to stand in light and pretend I'm not starving.

Turning toward home feels like a different kind of bravery.

Sam claps my shoulder once—gentle, steady.

"Come on," he says. "Let's sleep. Tomorrow we send the masters. Tomorrow we keep moving."

We walk back to the motel room. The streetlight flickers behind us, stubbornly trying to stay lit.

As I walk inside, I look at Zoey's message one more time.

Call when you can.

I don't call.

Not yet.

I turn the phone face-down and let the secret sit between my ribs like a second heartbeat—dangerous, insistent—promising everything and guaranteeing nothing.

Track 10 — New Jersey & Florida

Second-day air on a package from New England.
Someone took the time so you would be the only one who knew.
There are spaces between New Jersey and Florida.
There is a difference between black and white.
A story held together by a spine.
When you are let inside, know the difference—hold on tight.
A bottle of red can't be known until you uncork it.
Then you let it breathe.

The road is mostly space.

That sounds obvious until you live inside it—until you realize how much of your life can become the in-between. Not the stage. Not the nights you can post and point to as proof. The gray stretch between: hours where nothing happens except time passing and your thoughts getting loud.

If the highlights of my career are a handful of nights—small rooms that felt briefly holy—then the weight of it is everything around them.

New Jersey and Florida.

Not always literal. Not those exact places. More like coordinates on a map of distance: the long span between one life and another, between who you are and who you keep trying to become.

We leave before dawn because the next gig is far enough that we

TRACK 10 — NEW JERSEY & FLORIDA

have to treat the highway like a job. The blue Chevy G20 is packed tight—two acoustic cases, a duffel of cables, a bin of merch, blankets shoved into the back so the plywood platform looks almost intentional. Sam drives with his shoulders slightly hunched, coffee balanced in the cupholder like a fragile promise.

I sit in the passenger seat with my laptop open on my knees and my phone face-up beside it, trying to look like a person who can multitask without unraveling.

Kate said tomorrow.

Tomorrow is now.

The masters are on a hard drive in my bag—files that contain my throat, my hours, my stubbornness. I've listened to them so many times I can't tell anymore what's good and what's only familiar. I've made tiny edits in motel rooms, in the van, in the back corners of venues while Sam watched a stage get assembled for someone else.

I plug in the drive and start attaching files to an email like I'm offering pieces of my body.

Subject line. The smallest battlefield.

I type it once, delete it. Type it again. Everything reads either too hungry or too cold.

Finally, I choose the safest version of myself:

Masters + Live Clip

I attach three tracks. One live video from the showcase that doesn't make me cringe. Then I write the note—short, competent, trying not to kneel.

Kate—

Thanks again for last night. Attached are three masters and a live clip. Let me know if you need anything else from us.

Best,

Miles Skye

I stare at it, waiting for my stomach to stop twisting.

Sam glances over without taking his eyes off the road. "You send it?"

"Not yet."

He nods like he expected that.

"You want to count to three?"

"Don't."

"I'm serious," he says, a faint smile at the corner of his mouth. "Count. Then send. You can't negotiate with your own fear forever."

I exhale and hit send.

The email disappears. The van keeps moving. The world doesn't change.

That's the quiet cruelty: you can do a brave thing and the universe still looks bored.

We cross into another state. Signs change. The radio fades in and out. The heater coughs warm air that smells faintly like old coffee and road salt. Outside, the landscape shifts from bare trees to industrial sprawl and back again, as if the country can't decide what it wants to be.

At 9:17, my phone buzzes.

My body reacts before my mind can catch up.

Email. Kate.

Subject line: *Dates + Terms (Tentative)*

Hope does the stupid leap it always does, like it hasn't learned a single lesson.

I open it.

It's business. Two dates in March. A venue name I recognize—small but respected. A number that won't rescue us, but might keep us afloat. Requirements: promo assets, press photo, a short bio, social support.

Social support.

What I need isn't likes. It's rent.

Near the bottom she writes:

Need confirmation by end of week.

If you can't lock it, I'll fill the slots.
No hard feelings—just timing.
End of week.

The window is closing, and she says it the way professionals say anything sharp: clean, reasonable, inevitable.

I read the email twice. The words don't change. The pressure does.

"That a yes?" Sam asks.

"It's... terms," I reply.

He glances over.

"Which means?"

"Which means it could be real if we don't screw it up," I say, and I hear the mania in my own voice.

Sam nods once.

"Okay. What's the catch?"

I read him the end-of-week line.

He makes a sound that is half laugh, half fatigue.

"Of course it's by end of week."

We drive in silence awhile, letting the weight settle between us like a third passenger.

There's a difference between black and white.

This is the difference: not fame, not failure—just a long gradient of partial visibility. Half-doors. Almost. Maybe.

I've lived in the maybe for so long it feels like a permanent address.

At a gas stop, Sam fills the tank while I sit on the curb and scroll the email again, as if rereading it might reveal a hidden kindness. My fingers are numb from the cold. My chest is tight from the fear of being hopeful. Sam returns and hands me a water.

"We can do it," he says, practical. "But we have to talk money."

Money. The word lands like a dull object.

March isn't just a date on a calendar. It's gas, hotel nights, food, strings, repairs, the risk of saying yes to one thing and losing another.

Survival is algebra you do in your head while pretending you're chasing art.

Back on the highway, it hits me: I haven't told Zoey.

I told her I missed her. I told her it was a long day. I did not tell her the reason my blood is singing and sick at the same time.

Because telling her turns this email into a promise. And promises are the thing I keep placing in her hands like weights.

My phone buzzes.

Zoey.

You okay? Haven't heard your voice in a while.

I stare at the message until my throat tightens. I imagine her house back in little Rhody—our little Rhody, small enough to feel like an anchor even from hundreds of miles away. I imagine her moving through rooms where my absence has become a familiar shape.

I call.

She answers on the second ring, breath soft, guarded.

"Hey."

"Hey," I say. "You got a minute?"

"Yeah," she replies. "I'm on break."

I could tell her cleanly. I could tell her carefully. I could tell her in a way that doesn't ask her to carry it. Instead, I start with the safest part.

"We had a good night," I say. "A listening room. Kate was there."

Zoey is quiet.

"And," I add, feeling the lie loosen, "there might be something in March."

"Might," she repeats.

"Yeah," I say. "Two dates. Not locked. But… terms came in."

A pause. Long enough to hear the air between us.

"That's great," Zoey says finally. The words are correct. The tone is cautious, like she's stepping around broken glass.

"I know," I say. "I'm excited."

"I'm happy for you," she replies, and I believe she means it. That's what makes it hurt. "Just—"

"Just what?" I ask, too quickly.

"Just don't make me hold it if it's not real, okay?" Zoey exhales. "I can't—" She stops. "I can't do the whiplash anymore."

My stomach drops.

"I'm sorry," I say.

"I'm not trying to be mean," she adds quickly. "I'm just tired, Jude."

Tired again. The climate of us.

"I know," I whisper. "I'm tired too."

Silence.

Then she says, softer, "I miss you."

"I miss you," I say back, and for a moment the road goes quiet inside my chest.

"I have to go," she says. "Break's over."

"Okay."

"Be careful," she says.

"Yeah. You too—sorry," I say, and hate the reflex.

After the call ends, I stare out the window at the blur of winter landscape and feel the contradiction sharpen: I'm chasing rooms while the person I love is learning how to live without me.

There are spaces between New Jersey and Florida.

There are spaces between Miles-the-singer and Jude-the-man. Between what I'm building and what I'm breaking.

Sam breaks the silence.

"We confirm?" he asks.

"End of week," I say.

"Yeah, but..." He glances at me. "Do you want it?"

The question is simple. The answer isn't.

I think of the venue. The press. The possibility.

I think of Zoey's voice, careful with hope.

I think of the G20—our little blue lifeboat—eating miles like it's starving.

I think of Rhode Island: salt in the air, the idea of home, the life that stays put.

And I hear myself say, honest and scared:

"Yeah."

Sam nods once.

"Okay," he says. "Then we do the work. We make it real."

The road keeps stretching. The day keeps moving.

And somewhere in the long spectrum between black and white—somewhere in the space between New Jersey and Florida—I feel the faintest shift: not salvation, not a breakthrough—

just the smallest sensation of the road changing its meaning.

Track 11 — Frozen Desire

I live in the season that refuses to thaw.
Numbness, dressed as discipline.
I drink to make the world softer,
and the world becomes a fog I can't return from.
Still, your name stays sharp in my mouth—
desire, frozen and faithful.
The heart doesn't ask permission.
It simply bleeds.

The gig that night is good in the way good things can still feel thin.

A listening crowd. Warm lights. A room that hushes at the right moments. Sam and I play stripped—two acoustics, our breaths in the same tempo. The set holds. A chorus lands. People clap like they mean it. A few come up afterward and use words like *real* and *honest* as if they're handing me coins.

And still, when it's over, the familiar hollow returns.

Because the room empties. Because the night ends. Because applause doesn't follow you home—it follows the next band.

Outside the venue, the air is sharp. Winter has no patience for romance. We pack the G20 with the practiced movements of men who've done this too many times to pretend it's new: cases, cables, merch, blankets shoved back into their corners. The van door slides shut with a heavy, final sound—like a period at the end of a sentence.

Sam checks his phone.

"There's a bar next door," he says. Casual, but I can hear the fatigue underneath.

"We should drive," I reply automatically. "We've got miles."

"Yeah," he says. "But we're also human."

That's the trouble: human needs don't care about mileage.

We go in.

The bar is small and dim, the kind of place where the TV is always on and nobody's watching. The air smells like old wood, spilled beer, and a cleaner that can't quite win. A few locals sit near the end of the counter, laughing too loud at something that isn't funny. The bartender looks like he's seen every version of a man trying to forget himself.

We order whiskey because it feels like adulthood and punishment in the same sip.

The first drink warms my throat and makes my body unclench. The second takes the edge off the room. The third makes the silence inside me soften, and that softness is seductive.

Sam talks about logistics—March dates, gas, hotel points, the spreadsheet in his head that keeps us alive. I nod and answer, but my mind keeps drifting back to Kate's email like it's a candle I can't stop staring at.

Dates + Terms.

End of week.

Press.

A real room.

The language is clean, practical. And it hooks something primitive: the part of me that wants to be chosen. The part that wants to be lifted out of the *maybe* and placed, finally, into a sentence that ends with *yes*.

My phone sits on the bar beside my glass. The screen is dark, but it feels alive—an animal that might wake at any moment.

TRACK 11 — FROZEN DESIRE

A notification flashes.

Not Kate.

A comment on a clip. A stranger using a flame emoji like it's prophecy. Another follower. Another pellet of visibility.

The hit lands anyway. My body doesn't care where the recognition comes from; it just wants the chemical relief.

That's the frozen desire: not for a person, but for the feeling of being seen. Not love—attention. Not intimacy—proof.

Sam notices me staring.

"Don't do that," he says quietly.

"What?"

"Turn your life into a slot machine," he replies.

I laugh, but it's a tired laugh.

"It already is," I say.

Another round appears—two fresh pours set down with a practiced hand. Sam didn't order out loud. The bartender didn't ask questions. The drink is simply there, like the road: offered, easy to accept.

We drink.

Drink another.

The phrase returns like a dare.

Because alcohol is the simplest way to be off-duty.

Not to replace Zoey with another body—that would be too cinematic, too clean. No, I replace her with numbness. With the bar's low light. With the temporary sensation that my heart isn't carrying two lives at once.

A text comes in.

You still up?

My chest tightens. I stare at the words—the small domestic tenderness of them—and feel a heat of guilt. She's reaching for my voice and I'm sitting here letting whiskey erase the parts of me that would answer honestly.

Sam watches my face.

"Zoey?" he asks.

I nod.

"You gonna call her?"

I hesitate. The bar noise swells around me. A laugh cracks from the corner like a glass breaking.

"I don't want to dump this on her," I say.

Sam doesn't argue. He just looks at me the way he looked at me when we were teenagers and I was about to do something stupid: like he's trying to keep me alive without humiliating me.

Then he sets his glass down—decisive, the sound clean against wood.

"Then don't dump," he says. "Just… be present."

Be present.

The simplest instruction. The hardest one.

I type back with my thumbs hovering like they're afraid of honesty:

Yeah. Just got done. You okay?

The reply comes quickly, as if she's been holding her breath.

I'm okay. Miss you.

Miss you.

The words land like a hand on my chest.

I almost call. I almost stand up and walk out and drive back to Providence on sheer guilt.

Instead, I take a sip.

It's ugly, the way I can love Zoey and still choose avoidance. It's uglier that the avoidance feels like relief.

Sam finishes his drink and stands.

"We should go," he says.

"Yeah," I answer, though my body wants one more. My body always wants one more.

Back in the motel room, I lie on the bed fully clothed, shoes still on, staring at the ceiling. Sam takes the other bed and falls asleep

TRACK 11 — FROZEN DESIRE

quickly—his gift, his superpower.

My phone glows in my hand.

Call when you can.

Call. Again.

I don't.

I scroll instead—clips, comments, proof. Little bites of recognition that don't ask anything of me except to keep performing.

Then I open the Notes app and type without looking, because my hands are honest when my mouth isn't:

Drink another.

Replace my lover.

The words sit on the screen like a confession I can't take back.

I don't delete them. I don't even correct them. I let them exist, because some part of me needs to see the truth in black and white.

This is what chasing does to a person.

It turns desire into something preserved and hard. It freezes it into appetite. And appetite doesn't build a home—it builds a hunger that keeps moving.

In the early hours, I drift into sleep and dream of stage lights as candles, wax running down the spine of a book I've been carrying for years. In the dream, I try to wipe the wax away, but it only smears. The title disappears. The pages stick together.

When I wake, the room is gray with morning.

Sam is already stirring. The road is already waiting.

And my throat—my stubborn inkwell—already tastes like the next thing.

Track 12 — Failing Heart

I have spent my kindness like it was endless.
I have held what was never mine to hold.
Now the window narrows, and the air grows thin.
Holding becomes a habit, then a sentence.
Something in me begins to fail quietly—
not from hatred, but from giving;
not from weakness, but from years.
And still, I am asked for more.

Mornings after drinking always feels like punishment designed by someone who understands irony.

The body wakes up before the mind, full of small alarms: dry mouth, bruised temples, stomach turning like it's trying to crawl out of you. The air in the motel room is stale, heated just enough to feel wrong. The curtains leak thin gray light, and the light has a moral quality to it.

Sam is already up, hunched over the little coffee maker, watching it drip like he's waiting for a verdict. He doesn't say *I told you so*. He doesn't have to. The silence does it for him.

"You okay?" he asks finally.

"Yeah," I say, because *fine* is my first language now. Then I add, more honestly: "Not really."

Sam nods once. He pours coffee into two paper cups, hands me one

TRACK 12 — FAILING HEART

like an offering.

"Today's gonna be numbers," he says. "And calls."

Numbers and calls. The two things that can break you quietly.

I sit on the edge of the bed and open my phone. Kate's email is still there, pinned in my brain like a thumbtack:

Dates + Terms (Tentative)
Need confirmation by end of week.
If you can't lock it, I'll fill the slots.
No hard feelings—just timing.

A professional sentence that somehow sounds like a threat.

Sam sits across from me with his cup, elbows on knees.

"We should run the math," he says.

I nod. The hangover makes every thought feel heavier, like it's wearing boots.

Gas for March. Hotels if we can't crash with friends. Food. Time off whatever side hustles we can scrape together. The risk of saying yes and then paying for it later—sick, broke, burned out.

And underneath all that math, the other math: what it costs Zoey.

Because Zoey is not a line item. Zoey is the life that waits. Zoey is the person who keeps holding the end of the rope while I keep running farther out.

My phone buzzes. I check it, then look at Sam.

"Zoey?" he asks.

"No," I say. "Not yet."

I know I need to call her. I know the call is overdue. I also know that calling her means stepping into the part of my life where I can't hide behind gear and miles.

I stand and go to the bathroom. The mirror is unkind. My face looks like it's been living outside. The fluorescent light buzzes faintly. The air smells like hotel soap and old heat. I run cold water, rinse, try to look like someone who deserves to be trusted.

When I come back out, Sam is scrolling, expression tight.

"If we do this," he says, "we can't be sloppy. We can't miss another gig because we drank too much. We can't let the maybe turn into self-sabotage."

He says it calmly, but I can hear the edge.

"I know," I reply.

He watches me for a beat.

"Do you?" he asks—not cruelly. Just honestly.

I don't answer, because the truth is uncomfortable: I've been treating myself like collateral damage in my own story.

I sit and dial Zoey before I can talk myself out of it.

She answers on the third ring.

"Hey," she says. Her voice is careful, like she's walking through a room full of glass.

"Hey," I say. "You got a minute?"

"Yeah," she replies. "I'm on break."

I swallow.

"I got the terms," I tell her. "From Kate."

Silence.

"Two dates in March," I say. "Not locked yet. End of week to confirm. Real room. Possible press."

I try to sound excited. I can't help it; the hope is in my blood like caffeine.

Zoey exhales.

"That's... good," she says, and I can tell she means it. I can also tell she's bracing.

"It could be important," I add. "It's not huge money, but it's—"

"Jude," she interrupts gently. "Can I ask you something?"

"Yeah."

"Are you doing okay?" she asks. Not about the dates. About me. About the person who keeps turning himself into an engine.

TRACK 12 — FAILING HEART

My throat is barely open.

"I'm tired," I admit.

"I know," she says. "But I mean… are you okay in a way that matters?"

The question hits my chest like a fist. The hangover, the road, the endless in-between—suddenly it all feels visible.

"I don't know," I say, and my voice cracks on the honesty.

Zoey is quiet for a moment. Then she says, very softly, "Your window is closing."

I go still. The phrase is too perfect. Too cruel.

"What?" I whisper.

"Not your career," she says quickly. "I mean… me. Us. I can't keep holding this, Jude. I'm… I'm tired."

There it is, clean as a cut.

"I'm tired too," I say, and the words feel pathetic because my tiredness is chosen. Hers is collateral.

"I'm proud of you," she says. "I really am. But pride doesn't make dinner. Pride doesn't come to weddings. Pride doesn't fix the sink. Pride doesn't sit with me at night when the house is too quiet."

I close my eyes and see the past like a memory you can smell: salt air, cold sidewalks, the small, stubborn comfort of home. I see Zoey in that home, moving through a life that keeps rearranging itself around my absence.

"I'm trying," I say.

"I know you are," Zoey replies, and her tenderness makes me feel worse. "But trying isn't the same as being here."

I grip the phone until my knuckles hurt.

"What do you want me to do?" I ask, and I hate the question because it sounds like I'm asking her to write my life for me.

Zoey softly exhales.

"I want you to stop asking me to understand something that keeps hurting me."

Silence pours into the line.

Outside the motel window, cars hiss past on wet pavement, each one carrying someone's ordinary day.

"I'm coming home after this run," I say. "For real."

Zoey doesn't answer right away.

When she finally speaks, her voice is quiet and steady.

"You always say soon."

"I know," I whisper. "I know."

A pause.

"I love you," she says.

"I love you too," I say, and it's true, and it's not enough.

"I have to go," she says. "Break's over."

"Okay," I reply.

"Be careful," she says.

"You too," I say again, because my brain keeps making that mistake, and because it's the only way I know how to say: *don't leave.*

The call ends.

I sit there holding the dead phone like it's heavier than it should be.

Sam doesn't speak for a long time.

"That sounded bad."

"It is," I say.

He nods.

"You want to confirm the dates?"

The question lands in the wreckage of the call. Career and love, stacked like crates in the back of the van, both threatening to crush something if they slide.

I stare at Kate's email again.

End of week.

Fill the slots.

No hard feelings.

As if feelings aren't the whole point.

TRACK 12 — FAILING HEART

"I don't know," I admit.

Sam leans forward, elbows on knees.

"Here's what I know," he says. "If you don't confirm, you'll hate yourself. If you do confirm and you keep living like this, you might lose her anyway. So maybe the real question isn't March."

I look at him, throat tight.

"What's the real question?"

Sam holds my gaze.

"Whether you're willing to change," he says. "Not your songs. Your life."

The line rings in me like a chord.

I open my notebook and write, because writing is the only way I know how to make pain useful:

Your window is closing—because I can't keep holding.
It's just a matter of time before my spirit breaks.
I'm older than my time and have to play all of the parts.

Sam stands, finishes his coffee, and starts packing with the efficient calm of a man who knows the road doesn't care about your grief.

I watch him for a moment, then stand too.

Outside, the blue Chevy G20 waits, faithful as ever.

The road is still there.

The question is whether I'm going to keep letting the road decide who I am.

Because a failing heart isn't always dramatic.

Sometimes it just gets tired of being asked to hold everything...

everything...

everything...

everything...

(*End of record.*)

(HIDDEN TRACK)

"Turn Around (Home Version)"

[Verse 1]
    I've learned the shape of morning in cheap rooms,
    a heater doing its best impression of grace.
    I wake before the alarm like it's danger—
    like opportunity has teeth and knows my name.
    I check my phone the way a man checks weather,
    hoping for sun in a screen's cold light.
    And every mile I call it "building something,"
    I leave you bracing for the night.

[Pre-Chorus]
    You say, *Drive safe,* like the road is jealous.
    I say, *You too,* like I don't know better.
    We speak in habits.
    We speak in damage.
    We speak in almost, and later, and never.

[Chorus]
    Turn around—

(HIDDEN TRACK)

not for their hunger, not for their praise.
Turn around—
for the life that kept your place.
If the door opens, I won't run through alone.
If it shuts, I won't call the silence home.
I've been chasing light that doesn't warm me—
turn around.
Let me learn you as my living.

[Verse 2]
I've watched a room clap like it means salvation,
then empty out like it never knew my face.
I've worn the smile that makes me look investable,
and hated how good I am at playing safe.
Kate texts in clean, professional weather—
Could. Tentative. End of week.
And I hold that "maybe" like it's medicine,
while you're holding everything I won't speak.

[Pre-Chorus]
You don't need a headline.
You don't need a halo.
You need a body in the doorway, saying, *I'm here.*
You need the sink fixed.
You need the quiet.
You need the truth without the souvenir.

[Chorus]
Turn around—
not for their hunger, not for their praise.
Turn around—

for the life that kept your place.
If the door opens, I won't run through alone.
If it shuts, I won't call the silence home.
I've been chasing light that doesn't warm me—
turn around.
Let me learn you as my living.

[Bridge]
I've spent my kindness like it was endless,
on strangers and stages and "one more song."
But love is not a waiting room.
Love is not a schedule you survive.
Love is a key that fits the lock—
and a hand that doesn't flinch when you arrive.
So here's my vow, in plain clothes, no spotlight:
I will stop making absence my alibi.

[Verse 3]
I want a small table. A steady hour.
Coffee that doesn't taste like leaving.
I want your laugh in the same room as my breath,
no screen between us, no myth I'm feeding.
I want to write without bleeding you into it,
want to sing without calling it proof.
I want to be a man you can lean on,
not a song that only tells the truth.

[Final Chorus]
Turn around—
not for their hunger, not for their praise.
Turn around—

(HIDDEN TRACK)

for the life that kept your place.
If the door opens, I won't run through alone.
If it shuts, I won't call the silence home.
I've been chasing light that doesn't warm me—
turn around.
I'm coming home.
I'm coming home.

About the Author

Kevin Haslam is a Rhode Island–based writer and multidisciplinary artist with a soft spot for New England atmosphere and sharp little human truths. He's the author of *Salinger in the Rye*—an Amazon bestseller in American Literature Criticism—and he writes literary fiction that's equal parts lyric and bite. A recovering rockstar (yes, really—The Parker Star Band), he still believes in rhythm, big feelings, and making something out of noise. He's also the co-founder of Yoonie Co., an independent creative studio producing original work across writing, visual art, and music. Learn more at:

You can connect with me on:
- https://houseofhas.com

www.ingramcontent.com/pod-product-compliance
Lightning Source LLC
LaVergne TN
LVHW041627060526
838200LV00040B/1467